WHO AM I ?

My Journey In Worship Leading and
The Lessons I've Learned

MERAMI

Who Am I? - My Journey In Worship Leading
And The Lessons I've Learned

For permission requests, please contact:
Merami at:
truly.merami@gmail.com

Published & Edited by Johna Hill of
Jae Consulting
jhillspeaks@gmail.com

Book Cover Graphic Design By
Chris Serra
distinguishedcreative.co

ISBN: 979-8-9938367-0-6

TABLE OF CONTENTS

DEDICATION

To all Worship leaders, pastors, and ministers, continue to serve God and the church with nothing holding you back.

PREFACE

The hardest question to answer in life is Who Am I? We all deal with who we are, what do we want to do, and who do we want to be? As a child, I was told I would be a Missionary, I would preach the word and travel the world. I like to travel, but packing and unpacking is so dreadful to me. I still dread even the thought. At the age of 3 or 4 years old, I discovered that I can sing. But it was at the age of 5 years old, where I started to really enjoy singing. Today, it's still a big part of who I am.

I was born in a small border town, Eagle Pass, Texas. I lived there until I was about 8.5 years old. My dad, a hardworking man, who worked 2-3 jobs at a time, to put food on our table, one day decided to move my mom, 2 older brothers, my twin sister and I to Sacramento CA, the place where my journey as a Worship Leader started.

I grew up in California for the majority of my life. By the age of 19, I was part of several worship teams and they each shaped me and molded me into who I am today. This book is about parts of my journey that I have traveled, but not the whole journey which is still unfolding as I continue to serve God; It's still unfinished. I still have yet to discover more in my journey and learn what life and my walk with Jesus will teach me.

In the meantime, I want to share with you the insecurities and identity crisis I faced in my life as a Worship Leader. Yes you read it right, I experienced as a Worship Leader an identity crisis! At one point in my journey it was difficult for me to understand or know who I was. I didn't understand the anointing, or the call of who I was to be- a Worship Leader who was free in God and who would live courageously, convicted and committed to a lifestyle of worship.

In this book, I will discuss learning experiences from when I first started leading on a Worship team to where I am today. My prayer for this book is to bring to light what we as Worship Leaders can face; the pressures of thinking we have to have it all figured out or have our lives be perfect. The congregations we serve see us and think because we are on the platform on a Sunday, our lives are perfect. Our lives are not perfect! We, like you, go through hardships, we go through moments of giving up, and in one way or another we have felt insecure, afraid, and even lost in our journey.

I'm here to remind you with my story, there's still hope!! God can still use you and I when we are wanting to throw in the towel, when we are feeling like we can't lead on a Sunday because we feel inadequate, or not good enough because of our insecurities and lack of faith that He can use someone like you and me. Broken, busted, and messy people. HE CAN and HE WILL!

Get cozy, grab a hot chocolate or your coffee as I share with you my story.

Merami

CHAPTER 1

The Encounter

"I believe in God not because my parents told me, not because the church told me, but because I've experienced His goodness and mercy myself."
I'm So Blessed -Daily Devotional.

On a Sunday after one church service, I was invited to attend a Worship Rehearsal by the Pastor of the church I was attending. It was my third or fourth Sunday of attending. The pastor told me "You have a beautiful gift and there's an anointing on you. I would like for you to come to the Worship rehearsal on Saturday". It was the beginning of 2007 and like all the other years, I was expecting 2007 to be the best one yet. I was so excited to see all that God had for me that year. I left that Sunday morning with so much enthusiasm as well as a little bit of hesitation. Saturday came, it was a cold winter morning and all bundled up with a sweater and jacket, I was excited and a little scared. My hands were cold, yet somewhat sweaty due to the nerves. I said to myself, "Get Ready!" I went to the rehearsal not knowing that my life that day would change and I would discover whom God wanted me to be! I would encounter God and my life would never be the same, my relationship with God would be intimately close.

A bit of my story: I grew up in a pentecostal church in Texas and started singing when I was 3 years old. We had church services Sunday morning and night. I would sing a special song every Sunday night for our testimony service. I remember little me, grabbing a mic and singing with my little feet planted on the carpet on the pulpit and singing "Jehova Es Mi Pastor" the first song I learned and first bible verse I learned all at the same time. I would sing that song every Sunday night. My mom told me one time, she remembers when I was a toddler, I was always singing. I was a songbird. She told me, "If you were not talking, you were singing." I believe it, because I remember when I was about 5 or 6 years old, my mom was recording a cassette on her cassette stereo which meant no noise was to be made because the recording would pick up the background noise. We still have the cassette to this day, and yup, you can hear little me whistling on tune and not staying quiet. There's a long clip of me whistling a tune on that recording. It's like at a very young age I knew I was a singer. The love for music grabbed me real young.

At the prominent Spanish Speaking church I attended at the time, during my beginning days of being on a worship team, we rehearsed and went over 5-6 Spanish songs with the musicians and singers and then went home afterwards. That was the "thing" to do when you had a worship practice. Most of the time, it would be a quick 1-2 hour kind of practice. It was not a common thing to experience God at our rehearsals, I was not used to having encounters with God at rehearsals like I did that Saturday morning in 2007. I was not even used to praying corporately for one another after a rehearsal. Usually the group members had to go home right after because they had prior engagements to attend to.

I remember having encounters with God at a young age, but nothing like this one. I remember when I was younger, being at the church I grew up in in Texas, we were singing the beautiful hymn which is still one of my favorites to this day, "Alleluia". I remember singing that hymn and my twin sister and I heard a choir of angels singing with us in the background. It sounded like a choir of many voices and languages singing with us. You can feel such a strong yet peaceful breeze in the air inside the building. I've also encountered God in my dreams before, but this encounter was so different, it marked me.

That rehearsal that one Saturday morning was different. We practiced the set for that Sunday (which was, the very next day). After we had finished, the Worship Leader told us to get on our knees and let God minister to us as we had already prepared for Sunday. I went to the center of the altar and knelt down and began to pray as the words of what I had prayed a few days back came to my memory. A few days before, I was in my room praying, feeling inadequate, alone and like my prayer was not reaching God. I felt like He had other things to do and was not listening. The words of "I need You, where are You? Can You hear me?" Little did I know, God would meet me where I was. Have you ever prayed to God so specifically, that your prayer is answered and you are left without words in amazement that He answered so quickly? That's what happened that Saturday morning.

Let me tell you, thinking about it today still moves me and brings tears to my eyes. It moves me, because God saw me. He met me right there. He held me. He reminded me that He has me. Then it happened, something I had never experienced. My whole body felt hot. I felt a fire in my belly. I was shaking and crying in His presence. I was laid out and it was like my face was eating the carpet. I was not expecting God to speak the way He did that Saturday morning. God spoke to me so clearly through Christine, a close friend of many years. God places people in our lives to push us to be whom we are created to be in Him and for Him. We need friends like that. Friends who believe in you, and bring out the best of you. Those are the kind of friends I have today.

God will use those He has placed in our lives- as I like to put it, "To snap you back to reality" when you don't want to face it. God used Christine to speak in my life. Our friendship was one of kindred spirits. Since day 1, God used her to speak, not what I wanted to hear, but what I needed to hear. Many times, I didn't like or even wanted to face the truth that was staring me in the face. It was the truth of God's word that set me free in those times and still frees me today.

She was the friend who, for many years, prayed for me, prayed with me, cried with me, encouraged me, and celebrated so many of my joyful moments. She stood with me in the trenches -and there have been many. I'm very selective with my friendships. I don't open up easily. You might befriend me quickly, but it takes a while for me to truly trust. I have a guard up, and it's not easy to break through.

My guard is up because I have been hurt and I'm still working on letting it down and trusting with my heart. That wasn't the case with Christine. She befriended me easily and I did as well. Over the years, our trust grew and we became more like family. Her family is so dear to my heart.

That Saturday, God used her to remind me of my calling. The week leading to the encounter, I struggled with so much anxiety and fear. I prayed that week and asked God, Why me? You chose me for this?! What am I called to do? Do you hear me? Are you even there? Why is everything in my life a mess? Why are you punishing me? Hello, are you there? I was waving at Him like those blow up figures you see move in front of a store when the wind tosses them all around. That was me. I was trying to get

God's attention. That was my heart's posture and questions I had been battling a few days before. As I was on my knees in the middle of the altar, I could not pray. I had a cottonmouth and words could not nor would not come out. It felt like I had eaten a whole cochinito (Mexican pan dulce) and needed a glass of milk to wash it down. Or when you eat black licorice and you can't find water fast enough to wash it down because the taste is not good in your mouth. I knew people were there, but it felt as if they dissipated. It was me and Jesus at the altar. In front of me were the instruments. The piano on the far right and the drums on the far left, and in the middle were the microphone stands. My eyes tightly shut, my head bowed down trying to express words- I wanted and I needed for Jesus to listen and respond. I remember in my mind, thinking this is pointless. I was so wrong. It was not pointless, it was intentional. Jesus was intentional. He responded in a personal way. I had not told anyone what I was going through, or how I felt or even what I had prayed.

Right there, God grabbed a hold of me, and grabbed my attention. I jumped when I felt someone touch my shoulder and started to speak a spiritual message to me later realizing it was Christine. The words shook me, there was a power and authority that came out of her mouth, that it felt like it was God speaking through her. The encounter was so personal, so intimate. I am reminded of it when I have wanted to let go of the passion and calling. I go back to that day of me being marked by His presence.

That day, He placed a fire, a stirring inside my heart and my spirit that has made me the Worship Leader I am today. One that is not just passionate to sing, but loves to see when God moves in the hearts of His people. I love it when God takes over and overwhelms you in a place where we are all gathered together singing and praising His name.

Before I had this encounter with God, I was not aware of the anointing I carried. I didn't know there was an anointing, a power inside me. I had not yet tapped into what was inside of me just yet, or maybe I just had tapped the surface. Before that life changing encounter, it was a normal thing to sing every Sunday and leave the same way I came. There was no change. It was mundane. I got comfortable with it being the same. It was routine, and it was like that for years. I was so used to the singing but not the ministering part of being a worship leader.

I was told time and time again, "Wow there's something about your voice when you sing. You can feel God's presence and you have a strong anointing". Hearing that at the age of 19, I did not understand it or believe it. All I knew was that I could sing. To me, I had a beautiful voice and that was it, That's all I knew. Deep down inside I knew there was something in me but I did not know what it was. I questioned it. What is it? Why me? How? I didn't know why, let alone believe why God had given me this talent, at the age of 3 years old.

At 3 years old, I would sing a special during the service and at the end of each Sunday night, my madrina (god-mother) would give me $0.25. Yep I was given a quarter every Sunday for singing. But honestly, I didn't like the idea that I was earning money to sing. I enjoyed singing but I didn't want to make money off of it. That was never my focus. Even at 3 years old, I didn't like getting that quarter. I felt like I was being showcased and that was never my heart. I sang because I enjoyed singing. I loved & still love to sing about who God is.

I never made it a career or went to school for music. It was a God given talent. I take vocal lessons now because I have learned that we need to develop our gifts. Also there have been a couple of times where I have lost my voice due to physical issues. I had a scare where I thought my vocal chords were damaged. I had been singing incorrectly for a long time. I wasn't breathing and using my diaphragm. I was actually shouting. I never took a singing lesson growing up. I started singing on a Worship team when I was a pre teen, and I began to lead worship in my early twenties. But I didn't know that you needed to use your diaphragm and not your throat to sing.

The Encounter I experienced that Saturday in 2007 at the age of 23, ignited a passion inside of me for not just Worship, but for His presence. I was in awe of how God responded to my questions, the ones I had prayed for a couple nights ago. As I laid there in His presence, I was speechless and at the same time, I felt God's love. I felt the love of a Father, the kind where you can just sit on Daddy's lap and talk to Him. I felt an overwhelming warmth, a hug from my Heavenly Father. He knew, God knew how I felt, He was involved and interested in me!

That day, I made a decision, I would be open with God, and pour out my heart to Him as His child. I was left in awe of knowing that God was there. I felt like a little kid being picked up by their Father and taken by His hand to go on a journey with Him. It would be a ride of a lifetime. I felt His embracing love. As He answered me, "Yes I care about you, I am not punishing you, but I am preparing you for something greater! Yes I hear you, Yes I am Here!" It was so personal. So intimate. God met with me. That encounter changed my life forever. The encounter did not end there, I have and continue to experience God in an intimate way. This encounter though, marked my life forever.

CHAPTER 2

After The Encounter

"I am anointed to accomplish my assignment"
Isaiah 61:1 Pinterest post
by Kay Turner

You're probably wondering, "So what happened after the encounter?" As they say, "One Encounter with God, changes you! Yes, I was not the same person. It was not just that one encounter, there were many. My heart and passion for worship ministry grew deeper as time passed. I experienced God move in me, and through me as He used me to sing and bless His people with the gift He had given me.

Sunday after Sunday, God showed up, set lives free and brought healing. I remember there were some Sunday services, where the Pastor could not even preach because of God's presence being so strong in the building. During that season in my life, I got to see my calling develop and God pour His anointing over my life as well.

Not only did I experience God's presence in my room, but God gave me prophetic dreams. He spoke to me in my dreams, and showed me what He wanted to do in my life. One dream that is still vivid in my mind and in my heart is me leading worship on a Sunday at a church and the presence of God being so tangible, so real in that place, that when I was done ministering oil was dripping off me, (The Holy Spirit). I remember the morning waking up after having that dream, shaking, sweating and my legs feeling wobbly, trying to walk and feeling like I was going to fall on the side of my bed. I wrote it down in my journal and went on with my day after I was able to compose myself, not knowing that years later this dream would later be confirmed by one of the members on the worship team who I would serve alongside.

There was also a time where melodies would come to mind, and later words were put to those melodies but were never recorded professionally. A friend of mine did add some guitar riffs to one of the songs and it was recorded on my phone and I sent it to my email. It's kept in my files. To this day, I have not revisited that song. I still have some of the songs in a notebook today, but I don't remember the melodies.

Maybe one day, I will revisit the song and record it on Youtube but do not hold me to it! It has never been a dream of mine to record an album. I have been approached to record one by a close family friend and my dad has told me I should record an album. My answer to that has been and still is- if in the future, If I were to ever collaborate or record with someone, I am open to do so. Don't get me wrong, I love to sing and I love music. I just never saw myself as a recording artist. I saw and still see myself as a Worship Leader. A Levite, someone who ministers to the church and God's people. My heart is for the souls, it's about God reaching souls that walk through those doors every Sunday morning, broken, lost, and in need of Jesus as their Lord and Savior.

The encounters in that season, I had in my prayer room, in the secret place, were my training ground. The place where God shaped me, where He transformed me, where He poured not just His love but poured His anointing on me. It was in His presence where I learned to bring what I experienced in the secret place to the platform on

Sunday. It was what prepared me to sing what God placed in my heart to sing. It was those moments that marked my life and still do. In my secret place, I built and continue to build a relationship with the Holy Spirit. In building a relationship with the Holy Spirit, I have discovered spiritual gifts and God uses me through them. I discovered the gift of discernment, and word of knowledge and still use the gifts today when The Holy Spirit leads me. I can depend on the Holy Spirit and His leading and draw from that well to pour out on Sunday. I have also discovered that the prophetic songs God has given me to sing, have been for that precise moment. Those songs are declarations of my private encounters with God. The faithfulness and goodness of God I have experienced in my time alone with Him have turned into songs I have sung in a Sunday service that have gotten me through hardships and I have experienced God move in those Sunday services.

Through the encounters and the dreams I had during my beginning years as a Worship Leader, I learned to trust God with the gift He had given me. I realized that this was not something given to me but there was a responsibility that came with it. I was just not gifted in singing but I was anointed to reach souls. That was, and still to this day, is my assignment. It is more than singing and doing it well, it's about God and what He has for His people. That is still the goal and my heart's desire every week I step on a platform. I still think about and pray for the souls that will be there every Sunday. I pray for God to reach them, and for them to have an encounter that will change their lives, that will set them free from bondage, and empower them for the week they are going to face. It is true, an encounter with God can change anything. It can change you, it can set you free, it can empower you to do what God has called you to do.

What happens after the encounter? It seems simple, but it comes with a heart that is willing and open to receive what God has- the very moment we encounter His presence. Change. We become new in Him. That is what happens. Once you encounter Jesus, you will never be the same again. Not saying you won't go through hardships, because you will, but it's the encounters, the intimacy with the Holy Spirit that will help you through those times. We are constantly changing and going from Glory to Glory.

It comes with a big responsibility. It is something I do not take for granted, but hold onto. The times I spent in His presence and keep spending in His presence is what I will never trade. If it was not for the encounters; the precious empowering moments, in His presence, encountering Jesus and Him meeting me right where I was (and where I am) in my journey with Him, I would not be where I am in my life or have the courage to write this book. It is all because of His presence, that I can share what I have learned, what I have faced, and how His presence has been the key to my freedom, to my safety, and my security in Him.

CHAPTER 3
The Crushing

"When we are crushed like grapes, we cannot think of the wine we will become." Henri Nouwen

Many want the calling, the anointing, the gifts but don't want to go through the process of the crushing. At a time in my life, I had to realize and quickly step into the responsibility and understanding that it was more than just song selection and going to rehearsals. I had to go deep with God. Deep not just in His word and prayer, but deep in myself even when I didn't want to face the real me. My true self would blossom and my fruit would be recognized. I had to go through the winepress, that's where the crushing of things in my heart-my inner being that needed to be crushed, were crushed, and out of that came not just anointing but fruit.

What is the crushing? Glad you asked. The way I will describe it is going through the process of a grape being squeezed, and crushed so that what's inside of you will come out and be poured out like wine. In order for new wine to be made, the grapes have to be squeezed and crushed. Just like the grape goes through the crushing and squeezing, we too will go through that process to get new wine. During the time when you're being crushed, it hurts, it is not comfortable, it shapes your character, your pride is tested. Yes, pride, your ego, whatever doesn't belong in you, your fears, your doubts, your insecurities to name a few, are all crushed and an anointing from that crushing comes out of you and pours through you.

I had to be poured out in the secret place in order to pour out on the platform. Many times, those long nights in His presence, Him shaping me, molding me, were not the easiest, or enjoyable (meaning the crushing), but it was and is still necessary for me to go through. It's not just a one time thing, I still go through the crushing. I go through it daily. I am not perfect, there are still things that I need to let go of and die daily. I still have to check my heart, my motives and not let fear overwhelm me. Fear of failure is and has been crushed in the crushing. I recommend that you do not go through this process alone, it is a lot easier when you have someone with you who can pray with you and hear you out when you need to talk about the process. Surround yourself with people who will not just see you through it, but pray you through it.

During that period in my life, I was not in a good place. I was a hot mess, I didn't think I was the right choice God made to choose to lead Worship. I doubted my calling. I doubted my capability to lead. I would think "You can't, you don't know how, you're not capable of doing anything". Because I thought I was not capable, God must have made a mistake in calling me for the Worship Ministry. I began to believe more what I thought about myself than what God says about me. I did not believe what God's Word said about me. I believed the lies of the enemy instead. Questions and thoughts would pop in my head like why me? What do I have that is so special to God? Who am I? Others can do it better than I can. My way of thinking led me to the comparison game. I would compare myself to other Worship Leaders. That was a hard chain to break, which I will go more in depth in Chapter 5.

In the crushing, God exposed me. He revealed things in my heart that needed to be mended and removed. He also crushed my doubt, my fear, and my mindset. I had a bad perception of myself. I did not believe in myself, I would belittle myself and allowed others to belittle me as well. In those long nights in His presence, during the process of the crushing, my character, my mind were transformed. I was challenged. Challenged to believe what I sang and the message of the songs. It took me a long time to believe what I sang and let God minister to me first, before the songs were ministered to the church, and the congregation.

As I went through this process, the songs I would lead on Sundays started to mean more than a melody, more than lyrics, they started to change me. The songs started healing me and restoring my soul. Something inside of me was being transformed. There was a deeper meaning to the songs and message of the songs. Little by little, I was building my confidence in God. I was learning what it was like to sing with authority! I began to listen to songs that didn't just have meaning but were scripture based. I even discovered my love for God's word. I realized why as a child, I knew and to this day, still go back to those bible verses and apply them to my daily life. It was a love for both God's Word and Worship. I still go to songs that are scripture based and let them wash over my mind, heart and spirit.

During the crushing, I was really blessed by songs from a couple of mainstream Worship artists. Well known artists like Israel & New Breed, Hillsong United, and the first couple of albums from Jesus Culture to just name a few. Songs like, "I Will Search", "The Stand," "Never Let Go,"and "Holy," these and hymns are songs that still move me and still minister to me. I can still listen to those songs and tag old hymns as I lead on a Sunday at church, and feel God's presence each time more intimately. They still take me back to that vulnerable place. The place where I first was crushed, shaped, molded, changed, and challenged. The place of the start of my journey as a Worship Leader. The place where I experienced His Presence and He became my best friend. He showed up in my room, and held me when I cried in His presence. He spoke to me and gave me dreams and visions of what my future would be. He showed me I will go to places and be His mouthpiece, His voice to those He sends me to. The crushing at that time, it hurt, I did not want to go through it but I now know, it was necessary. I needed to be crushed and reminded that He was preparing me for what my journey would be like today.

CHAPTER 4
Fear of Failure

"You fall, get up, make mistakes, learn from them, be human and be you" Priyanka Chopra Jonas

I struggled with thoughts that fed and led into my insecurities. I was afraid of falling flat on my face every Sunday service not literally but metaphorically. I was not confident in what I was doing. Before each Sunday service, I would think, "What am I doing?" Can someone else lead for me? I can't do this! Even when God would show up and it was a glorious service, I still questioned myself. I didn't believe in what God had given me. I didn't see what others around me saw, or maybe I was too scared to see what was placed inside of me because to me it was not perfect, it was flawed. Yes, I was scared. Fear and doubt tried to control me for a long time. I was always scared to step deeper in what God had for me. I was scared to lead and step into the prophetic. I doubted that God could use me and was scared to fail at everything I did. I was not secure in the gift or the calling God had given me. It was a rough time for me to lead at the beginning of my journey as a Worship Leader. I had stage fright.

This stage fright is the kind where my mouth gets dry, my legs shake, and I feel like I am about to throw up. Sometimes I wouldn't remember the service on a Sunday because it would be a blur. The lights and the height of the stage wouldn't help either, I would be blinded by the lights and the height of the stage made me dizzy. I am a short curvy woman and standing on the stage for long periods of time was uncomfortable. Especially when I wear wedge heels. My feet would hurt. I would get cotton mouth and I was drinking 2-3 water bottles at a Sunday service. I would close my eyes because I didn't want to see the people in front of me. That took awhile to get used to. When I messed up, or songs didn't come out like I'd expect, I wanted to quit. I would convince myself I was not cut out for this.

I remember when I first experienced fear of failure. I was in 2nd grade when we lived in a small town in Eagle Pass Texas. I attended the elementary school (Graves Elementary) that was less than a five minute walk from our house for my twin sister and I. I still remember the straight route we took every day from our house. My twin sister and I were in separate classrooms. I had the meanest teacher in all the school. Ms D. For privacy purposes, we will just call her Ms. D. She reminded me of a character from one of the scary books I read growing up. I don't recall the name of the book. In my 2nd grade kid's mind, she looked "intimidating". Ms. D, had long shining dark hair and her complexion was dark chocolate. Her eyes, big and brown. And were so much bigger when she would yell at you for not excelling in her class. She would always yell at her students when they didn't do well in an exam. I was one that she would yell at more times than I would like. She would yell the same thing, "Do better next time, or you'll regret it later!" That phrase left me traumatized. I was traumatized being in her class. I don't recall telling my parents, because I was so scared of the consequences. She was a scary, mean woman. I kept quiet and did my best to not get yelled at by her or get smacked by a ruler. She would slam the ruler on the desk too. The Texan school system was different from the system in California back then, but that's not what I want to talk about here. I didn't want to fail at anything! I had to be perfect and not get yelled at by her ever again. I studied hard because I had to get a passing grade on the next exam. I don't remember if I passed the next exam, all I remember is not wanting to fail at anything ever again. But as time went on and as I got older, fear of failure was still there in my life. It kept creeping up and it slowly became my kryptonite.

Over the years, I've realized fear of failure has stopped me from succeeding in other areas in my life. I have started but never finished things in my life. When God told me to write this book, fear of failure tried to creep in. I was so scared to look back at my experiences and journey. I even asked myself, who is going to read this? Will it even make sense? How will anyone relate to this? I had to cancel those thoughts and I told myself this is something you will finish. You will share your story.

Even in ministry, I have faced fear of failing. Fear of failing the team I lead, fear of failing in my own walk, fear of failing God. I wanted to be perfect and live a perfect life. However, I did fall, I made mistakes along the way, but I got back up and tried again even when I was afraid of the outcome. There has always been something inside of me that pushes me to not give up no matter what I face. No matter how many times, I doubted, there was a fire and still is a fire inside of me that keeps me strong and firm in Him. There is nothing that can ever tear me apart from God, His love, and His presence.

I have come to realize that we are not perfect, and we will never reach perfection. We all have fears, we all make mistakes, we all mess up and that's okay. What matters is how we deal with it and not let it hinder us, or stop us from moving forward. I'll admit it took a long time for me to come to that realization. I am no longer pressured into wanting to be perfect. I am flawed and I am okay with the beauty of my imperfections.

There was a time in my life where I thought that worship had to be perfect. What do I mean? Let me explain. If a Sunday service was not perfect in the sense of sound, vocals, team effort, I failed as a worship leader. I fought with my thoughts every Sunday before stepping on the platform that this had to be a glorious Sunday! If the congregation was not into the set list, it was my fault. I went by the reaction from the congregation and the song selection. I put so much pressure on myself that I didn't want to fail. I was so scared to fail. There were even instances where I had an emotional breakdown by all the pressure I put on myself. There were even times when I thought I was going crazy in wanting everything to be perfect.

I remember one particular time when the Worship Team and I were invited to lead worship at a church and I felt like I had failed after leading that Sunday because there was no response from the congregation. It felt like I was pulling teeth in getting them to worship. I lost it in the green room after we finished our set list! I felt like it was my fault, it was my responsibility to make sure things went smoothly. That Sunday, it flopped. I focused more on the people's reaction and not on what God would do through me. The fear of failure caused me to not believe in what God had placed inside of me. The anointing I carried. I questioned it when it didn't go how I'd like it to or expected a Sunday service to go. I felt like I had to be the same or better than everyone else. I was a failure if I was not on top of the leading game. It was a competition for me; it wasn't about being a team player or part of a team. In a way it was, "Merami and the band'. I dealt with that for a long time.

Over the years, I have learned that the pressure of leading worship doesn't fall on me or any of us who lead worship. We don't have to worry about the sound or the technical aspect of the service. God will always move and show up no matter what the structure is. God is looking for a willing and obedient heart to do what He has called us as Worship leaders to do. When we truly cast our cares on Him,

He shows up and cares for us. Also, it is not our responsibility to take them into the presence of God, we are called to minister to the needs of the church. We are called to be a Levite in the frontlines of the battle.

I remember one Sunday at the current church I led before the pandemic of 2020 hit, one of the pastors came to say hi to me and looked at me and asked me if I was okay. I answered, " I am so nervous. I don't know why I am, I lead all the time." She could see the nerves were eating me inside. Her response set me free. She said, "You're nervous because you care! If you didn't care, you would not be nervous, you would just be like okay, whatever, let it be just an ordinary Sunday. But you care so much and your heart is so pure in it that you don't want to just lead but you want to minister and you feel what the church is in need to receive." Yes!! That's exactly true! After that Sunday I looked at my calling, the anointing God placed on my life differently. Once again, I was reminded why I do what I do. Why I am called.

I still get scared. I am human. I am not perfect. However, I am no longer moved by fear of failure or controlled by it. I trust God to help me and guide me when given the chance to minister on a Sunday. It's no longer the thought or the feeling of leading Worship to be perfect. I no longer put that pressure on myself of looking for perfection, because it will never be, because I am not perfect! I'd rather strive to please God in my gift, my calling, and trust the anointing He has placed in me, than to make sure I do a great performance and compare myself or be compared to other worship artists and fail at what I am called to do.

With experience and practice you learn to not let it be perfect and it teaches you that "it's okay" for it to be messy just like life can be.

Not everything in life is perfect or turns out how we expect it to be. Trust me, it didn't take me overnight to come to this conclusion. It took me letting go of my expectations and trusting God to work in me and through me. Hence: The Crushing.

CHAPTER 5
Comparing Myself

"Confidence is not possible as long as we compare ourselves with other people." Joyce Meyer

As I kept walking on my journey as a Worship Leader in my early years, it was so hard to not compare myself or be compared to other people in the same position as me. I was compared to how I led worship and how I sang by other leadership in the church. The comparison led to questioning my identity. As a result, I dealt with an identity crisis which I'll go more into detail in chapter 9. Is that even possible? An identity crisis in the church? Yes. Stay tuned for more details. Back in the early 2000's, there was a movement going on around the worship world. It was the "Jesus Culture" movement. If you're familiar with Jesus Culture, then you know who they are and the movement. If you're not too familiar with who Jesus Culture is, let me explain. Jesus Culture is a worship band that came from Bethel Church in Redding California. The way they started is at a church service on a Sunday and a recording of the service was uploaded on YouTube. Jesus Culture is known for flowing in the Spirit and declaring prophetic words as they minister in their worship meetings. They were the band to look up to in leading prophetically. At that time it was something new, something fresh. I remember discovering who Jesus Culture was for the first time as I browsed through YouTube and the video titled "I Exalt Thee!"popped up on my suggestions for videos to watch. I watched the video while doing homework at the library in the Community College I attended at the time. I wanted to listen to music and that video caught my curiosity.

I was late in discovering Jesus Culture, most of my friends who are also worship leaders had already heard of them. I remember as I watched the video feeling God's presence so tangibly that I wept. The flow of the prophetic worship was so beautifully sung and played that I wanted to learn how to lead prophetically. I was in awe of this. I wanted to be the next Kim Walker! I began to study Kim Walker from Jesus Culture. The way she sang, the way she led, and her mannerisms. She was whom I turned to as my example when it came to leading. But the difference was that Kim Walker didn't minister in Spanish, so all the words she would sing, I would translate them to Spanish or make it up on my own when I would lead on a Sunday. It was a trend to lead like Kim Walker. At one point, later on in my journey, I was told by a pastor, "Channel your inner Kim Walker and sing like her". I was shocked and appalled at the same time. It was not the power of Kim Walker, it was the Power of the Holy Spirit that made the services glorious.

I also compared myself to my worship leaders on the worship team I was on. One of the team leaders was Christine. Her aunt was in charge of the team and Christine was starting out to lead worship at that time. I had been leading for a while but felt like I couldn't meet the pastoral expectations in my leading role. I was wrong in thinking that, because that was not the truth. It was all in my head. I had those thoughts about myself and I am embarrassed to admit now, it became a competition. Christine was the English Worship leader and I was the Spanish worship leader. I competed with her and the other leaders. If I didn't lead like them, it was not prophetic (well, that's what I thought). I had to up my game and show them I too can sing prophetic worship. For me it was like monkey see, monkey do, but who can do it better? It had to be me. I had to be the one that was better than my team singers. That feeling & mentality didn't last too long. God seriously had to deal with me and put me in my place!

So when it came to writing a new song, because everyone I knew who led worship also wrote songs, so I decided to write a couple. I still have them in a notebook today. I only added music arrangements to one of them. I only did it to prove to myself I can do what everyone else was doing at that time. I am not proud of my behavior but that's what I did to "compete". As I wrote more songs, I came to the conclusion, I am not a singer song-writer. I have a few unfinished songs and that's okay. I have come to terms with not going back to finish them. Songs, more like declarations come out when I am leading, declaring what my heart and spirit express, known also as a spontaneous song.

We are worship leaders. It's a ministry. It is not about comparison or competition with our team members. It's not about who can sing better, who can lead better, who can "flow in the Spirit " better. We can't compete and be on the same team. We are there for one purpose and that is to minister to the congregation. We as worship leaders, it is not about us! It has never been or will ever be about us. I am sorry to have burst your bubble, but it is the truth.

It's sad to say, but I've seen it in churches today. I've seen worship leaders being compared to other worship leaders on the same team. There's even a preference with the pastors when one worship leader is better than another worship leader on the same team. I have experienced it. I felt like I was always competing for the approval of my pastors and at times even the approval of the congregation. I have been told more than once, "I only like the worship when you lead." or even been told, "You have more anointing than so-and-so, and I like your leading better". That's a lot of pressure on someone. Comparing yourself or being compared to someone else, can mess with who you are. It can cause you to think that you're the only one who can and no one else can lead like you do. It causes you to feel like you're irreplaceable or indispensable. During that time, my dad would always tell me, "The church service will go on without you. You don't always have to lead and be there, that's why there is a team." I would get into yelling arguments with him because I wanted to be the best and no one could lead like me.

You begin to feel like if you're not there or can't be there to lead worship, it will flop, crumble, and the responsibility falls on you. The pressures we put on ourselves comes from the comparison and competition we have with each other. We are supposed to be on the same team. We are better together. We're to help each other be there for each other and uplift each other. When we do that, we take off the pressure of the competition and become a team. That is the goal when I am a part of a Worship Team. I want to be on a team that helps each other and supports each other. It's not a competition. It's teamwork. It makes the dream work. Something I have found now in serving at The Father's House in Elk Grove, California. It's an amazing feeling knowing you are on a team that supports you and encourages you. Something I will cherish for a lifetime and not ever take for granted.

CHAPTER 6
My Mentor, My Angel

"A mentor is not someone who walks ahead of you to show you how they did it. A mentor walks alongside you to show you what you can do."
Unknown

Linda Holloway was not just my mentor, she was a close friend. She was a spiritual mom to not just myself but to many. She passed away on October 25, 2015. This chapter is to honor her life and the wisdom she poured into my life. There are so many memories I hold dear to my heart and are just for me to hold onto. However, I will share a couple with you all. I remember meeting Linda at one of our Spanish Worship Team Rehearsals. I was in awe of her spirit. The way she had a joyful spirit. It was so evident she lived and breathed worship. I loved hearing her sing. Her voice was angelic with an anointing that broke chains and moved mountains. Her soprano voice was so powerful that you felt God's tangible presence. You felt God's embracing love when she would sing.

She always greeted you with the sweetest smile and warmest hug. She made you feel like you were one of her own. She poured out love, joy, and strength in the lives she encountered. She cared about our Worship Team. There were a few of us young women on the Worship team who were mentored by Linda. We each had a wonderful life changing experience and friendship with her. To us, she was Momma Linda. She always made sure you were okay and whatever she could do to help, she would help, lend a hand, support, and encourage you. She helped me with paying for one of the camps

I was going to attend to help with worship, but I was low on funds to pay for the camp.

I miss her so much. I think about the talks we shared, the joy she brought to my life. Her wise words she shared with me. I think about how she would always say, "You gotta live your life to the fullest and don't be afraid to try new things!" She would also say, "make sure you travel as much as you can and see and experience new places." I still have yet to travel to my bucket list places, but I hope to. During the time Linda mentored me, I worked for a Non-Profit Organization (NPO), focused on Disability Rights of California. I took the light rail train to midtown Sacramento Monday- Friday. I remember our morning calls, her sweet voice, her laugh, you can hear her smile on the phone and could tell she was always happy to hear about my morning as I walked nine blocks to work after being dropped off at the light rail station on 9th and K street. Time flew fast when I would be on the phone with her. Those nine blocks were so easy to walk and I looked forward to talking to Linda each morning. We would text throughout our day and on my way home from work, a 1.5 hour ride on the train, we would text and sometimes we would talk on the phone. Our talks were so encouraging and we always ended our conversations with a prayer or with " I'll text you later." The times when I was dropped off after work at the light rail station, we would talk, mostly about our day or what was on our hearts to share with each other.

She spoke life and wisdom when I needed to be uplifted when I struggled with feeling worthless or out of place. She encouraged me to believe in who I was in Christ. She believed I was in the place God wanted me to be and that He had a plan for me to flourish where I was planted. She saw hope when I didn't see it. She believed in me, when I couldn't or didn't want to believe in myself. She saw God's anointing on my life and the calling God placed in me. Linda lived and breathed Worship. It was a big part of who she was, It was her DNA. Even when she was battling an illness she never stopped worshiping. She always spoke the Word of God and you knew she believed God's Word. I'll never forget how one night Linda, Linda's daughter, and I went to visit our friends' church for a Worship night and on our way to the church, her daughter played Donnie McClurkin's music, and Linda with hands lifted so high inside the car, crying and singing "Great Is Your Mercy" and claiming her healing and victory over her illness. A beautiful memory which even now as I am writing about it, still moves me to tears. I'll never forget that moment with her. I'll always cherish it.

Linda did a couple of activities before she passed. One of the activities she did and she would always tell me how she loved it and I should try it; She loved to crochet. If she was still here, I would take a class from her to learn how to crochet. I still can learn, but I know it would mean so much more learning from Linda. Another activity she would do is host Bible Studies at her house with a group of women. If I am not mistaken, the last book she studied with the women's group was the book of Acts from the bible. She also taught small kids in her home, getting them ready for kindergarten. She taught the kids shapes, numbers, ABC's, colors, the basics. She invested in my life and the life of many others.

One night, Linda and her husband attended the Women's Ensemble concert when I was in the choir at Cosumnes River College. I was so nervous, because I had a solo and I felt like I was not going to do well. I was not mentally prepared and the nerves were taking over my voice. As you can see, being nervous was something I dealt with even outside of leading worship on a Sunday. I invited friends and family to attend the concert, but for some reason they could not attend. Linda showed up. She was my family. Seeing them there, cheering me on, and smiling as I sang my solo made me feel loved and supported. I don't recall what song I sang for my solo. I initially thought I'd kept the program flier but I didn't. That night, I sang my solo, and gave it my best effort and I did exceptionally well. After the concert, they both came up to me, gave me a warm hug and said, "Beautiful singing Merami, you did so good! So proud of you!"

I remember a couple of weeks before she passed away, I was talking to her on the phone, and I felt so strong in my spirit to share with her a song that to this day still impacts my life and ministers to my spirit. It's a song that I was introduced to when I was in the Masters Commission program. The song, "He Is" by Aaron Jeffery is a song that describes who God is according to every book of the Bible. It describes God's sovereignty, His love, and His power. If you haven't listened to it, I HIGHLY recommend that you do. I'll never forget the reaction in her voice when she called me after listening to "He Is". She told me that the song blessed her so much, she had to share with her daughters and her family. She sounded so joyful and I could tell she was weeping when she called me. Tears of joy! I can hear it in her voice. When I hear the song today, I remember her voice, shaky, but joyful. You know that moment when you're happy and you have no words to say and tears are streaming down your face and you feel an unspeakable joy? That's what I think she felt that day when she heard the song.

Linda's last wish was to see her loved ones one last time. I remember receiving a phone call from Christine, my bestie, asking me if I had talked to Linda that day, I told her I did and she was okay, Linda was fine when I spoke with her. Then Christine told me Linda was not well at all, and to call Linda's daughter. I had just talked to Linda that same day in the morning and she told me she would call me back because she was going to get some test results. I called Linda's daughter and by the sound of her voice, I knew something was wrong. She told me to come to her mom's house to spend my last moments with her. Hearing her say that to me, crushed me so much. I couldn't stop crying. I was not prepared to say goodbye to Linda. I still had so much to share with her.

I arrived at Linda's house, and it was an atmosphere of worship. Singing her favorite hymns and worship songs. Her close friends were there, her family was there. She was surrounded by love and singing. It was a beautiful worship service. The house was packed with not just members of the Worship Team, but other church members as well. Those whom she had impacted were there to spend their last moments with Linda. I walked in the room where Linda was in. She was in her bedroom, sitting up on her bed with the strength she had left in her to talk to her loved ones one last time, and pour into their lives. That's what she did. She embraced me and told me to always live my life to the fullest and to live it joyfully. To never give up, always try and trust God to do the rest. I didn't want to leave that room. I wanted to be there with her all night. I cried in her arms, told her I loved her and she said," I love you too my Merami. I'll see you again soon!" I gave her one last hug and walked into the closet of the room. After my moment with her, I called Christine to tell her Linda was saying her goodbyes and we both cried on the phone and told each other what Linda told us when we were sharing our last moments with her. We both were so crushed. Momma Linda was leaving us. I couldn't bear it. After talking with Christine, I went to the living room of the house and sat on the couch and wept until it was time to be dismissed from the gathering.

We celebrated Linda's life on November 3, 2015. The service was truly a beautiful celebration. It was held at New Season in Sacramento, California. The house was packed with her family and friends and those she touched and impacted were there too. The place was full of singing her favorite hymns and worship songs. There was also a video collage of memories she shared with her family and friends. She lived a beautiful life. She touched and impacted so many lives. She was so loved and she loved many. She was a precious jewel, a mentor, a sister in Christ, an amazing friend, a spiritual mother to many as well as myself. I will never forget you, my Angel. I will never forget your smile, your laugh, your warm hugs, the way you loved your family and friends, your words of encouragement. I love you and miss you so much Momma Linda. I know I will see you again one day. Thank you for sharing your life, your wisdom, your friendship with me. I'm truly grateful for your life. Until the day I see you again my sweet beautiful Angel, and my friend. Forever grateful for you and the imprint you left in my heart.

Love always,

Merami

CHAPTER 7
F. R. I. E. N. D. S.

"Friendship isn't about whom you've known the longest. It's about who came and never left your side."
Anonymous

I've had some amazing friends, over the years, some have remained, some are no longer in my circle and I have made new friends that I believe will last for a lifetime. It is said, "to have good friends, you must be a good friend." I agree with that. Out of the few, I will only highlight 4. The ones who have been there for me throughout the years. I want to dedicate this chapter to them. If it wasn't for them, I would not have written this book, or be where I am today. If I can use a word or phrase to describe each friend, I would use Family, Truth, Voice of Reason, and Encouragement.

The first word, Family, Christine, represents that in my life. I met her at a church picnic back in 2004. A mutual friend introduced us as I was leaving the park where the picnic was held. We became friends a couple of weeks after meeting. As time passed, we led worship together and were a part of a traveling ministry Double Portion. We had our share of moments in our friendship where we disagreed but we never stopped praying for each other even throughout the distance the disagreements caused. In the years that I've known her, we became closer and we considered each other family. I love her family like my own and she became like a sister. Her family became my family. Even her siblings consider me a sibling to them as well. To them I am the adopted Texan Mexican sister

Christine is like family because when mine wasn't able to be there for me, she and her family stepped up and lent a helping hand. She and her family helped me out when I had no way of getting to the church, they helped me with a ride and I also was there for them when they needed a helping hand. We both considered each other family. Although she's younger than me, she is so wise beyond her years. Christine and I were part of a worship team called Double Portion that traveled to different cities in California. Our friendship grew a lot those years and at the same time was challenged throughout the 2 years we were in the group. I got to see and learn alongside her how to lead a worship team. I saw the sacrifices and effort she and her family gave to the ministry. Christine, I am forever grateful to you and your family. You helped me through my first years of ministry as a Worship Leader. Your support to me in writing this book is immensely appreciated. Thank you!

The second word, Truth. Damaris brings that to our friendship. I met her at one of the churches I served at in 2016. At that time, she was dating the youth pastor, who she's married to today. She would visit on Sundays before attending her father in law's church. She's always been easy to talk to. Even when we wouldn't see each other on a Sunday, the next time she was there, we would pick up right where we left off.

When Damaris spoke truth to me, I accepted and appreciated her wise words. Yes there were times, I didn't want to hear it, but I listened and she pushed me to see my true self and work on the things I needed to work on. Even in the midst of writing this book, I had a few truthful conversations with her and as uncomfortable as it was, the truth I discovered about me, set me free! During one of those conversations, I found out she was told by a mutual friend before she met me that I was too much to handle and I was needy. That was a surprise to me when she told me that she was warned about me. What??? It was a shocker to me because I didn't know that I could be too much. Maybe I came on too strong at the beginning or maybe not. I don't think I did.

I must admit, I have become a bit conservative and not as spunky as I was before. I'm still finding that side of me again . The bubbly side, the outgoing me, the one that is carefree. It has taken having some deep conversations with Damaris to rediscover that side of me. Damaris has brought that bubbly side out of me a few times. I am still working on trusting those I work with in ministry. I'm grateful and feel so blessed having Damaris in my life. She has pushed me and encouraged me to keep moving forward. Our friendship is one of uplifting in prayer through the losses and defeats and celebrating each other through the victories of life.

We send each other words of encouragement through text. We also check in from time to time to see how life is going for us both. She, too, was so excited and encouraged me to write this book. She'd check in to make sure I was still writing. Damaris, I am so blessed to have you in my life. You truly have been there when I did not know what I should do in my transitional period. You made sure, my gift, my calling, my assignment, was not done and I was still serving and not getting comfortable with online services during COVID. I thank God for your friendship. Thank you for pushing me to not just write my story but for helping me get me to a place to be fearless in my vulnerability. Te aprecio y quiero mucho!

The third one is Voice of Reason. Marysa and I have been friends since we were both 15 years old. Her mom worked with a few of our mutual friends and that is how she came to church. Her mom was invited by a mutual friend to come to one of our Summer events. We met the summer of June 1999 for our Youth Compel Night and a sisterhood was formed. It was a few of us girls that befriended Marysa. We all became really close. We would all ride in the same car and would stay up late after youth service. Our favorite place to go at the time was Mr. Perry's. If we weren't there, we would go to the Garcia family's house and stay up late playing dominoes or Uno.

Our friendship has been one of heart-to-heart talks about anything and everything. We grew up in the same youth group. She was and has always been one who has made me think after talking with her. I have left many conversations with her not only encouraged but enlightened. We have had many talks about this book and what I wanted to share and expect from this book. She helped me with being vulnerable while writing this book. When I told her she was in the book, she was happy about it and when I told her what word I used to describe our friendship, she agreed and laughed. We both did. I know Marysa will be in my life for a lifetime. She's one I know will always be in my corner cheering for me. I know distance is not an impediment, even when she has been away in the US Army

Forces serving our country, we have always made sure we connect either before she leaves, or when she comes back. We talk on the phone for hours about life and what goals we have for the year.

Marysa has shown me through her life experiences that we are stronger than we think and there is a fighter inside each and every one of us. She also has shown me to always follow your instincts. She has been through so much these past couple of years and it's been her strength and her faith in God that has been so impactful to me. I know there have been many times she's wanted to give up because it has been a hard journey, but her tenacity has left me speechless and in awe.

I'll never forget how one night we were supposed to go to the gym in downtown Sacramento, but I ended up having a crying sesh in her car in the downtown parking garage. Her words and insight on what I was going through that night was something I needed at that moment. God knew I needed my friend that night and I am so glad she was and continues to be there for me. We didn't go to the gym, we ended up going to our favorite spot, Denny's. Till this day we have our Denny's hangouts or just have our talks and then our infamous car selfies for Instagram. Which is mostly me posting. She is not too much into the social media craze.

Marysa, if it wasn't for our long talks in your car and your encouragement and wise counsel this book would probably not have happened. Thank you for being my ride or die. Thank you for believing in me and for all these years of wonderful blessings and memories with you. I love you! I'm looking forward to our Golden Girl days!

The last word, Encouragement. Paola. I met her at one of our Double Portion camps (DP) the summer of 2012. The camp was for 4 days. From Thursday evening to Sunday afternoon. We were talking outside at the bond fire worship service about life and God. We both encouraged each other. We talked about the service we just had that night and how God moved in our lives and how something in us changed and brought us deeper in God. We kept in touch after meeting at DP camp. She attended a few of our Worship Nights and events we had in the Bay Area. We added each other on Myspace and Facebook, exchanged phone numbers, became close friends and talked and texted very frequently. We still do today. When we talk on the phone, we always end up praying for each other and encouraging each other.

I'll never forget how during one of our phone conversations, she mentioned an experience she had recently gone through and how it was so hard to express it to anyone because she felt like she would be judged. I reassured her that it will never be the case with me. I will never judge my friends, that's never been a part of my character. I may have been judged in the past, but I will never be the one who points fingers at your mistakes. I will not condone your behavior but at the same time I will help you be restored and welcome you with open arms. Isn't that what the Bible says, to uplift each other and not judge? That's what I did, I was there for my friend Paola. I've even done that for friends who are not too close to me. I am the kind of friend who supports you and never once makes you feel like crap when you have failed or made a mistake. I am there and will be there for you in the trenches of life.

Loyalty and grace are the qualities I have learned in my friendships with the close friends I mentioned here by name. I have made mistakes, I have even wanted to give up and throw in the towel but their support, their love, their example of Christ in my life has and continues to help me keep pressing forward. Because of hurt and fear of rejection, I have not or don't always show you who I am. Only a selected few including these four individuals have seen/known the real me. They have seen me at my best and at my worst. They can see when I am okay and when I am not. Being vulnerable left me wounded in the past and if I could avoid it, I would. However, I have learned that vulnerability is not something I should shy away from or be afraid to share my heart but open up and not be scared of rejection.

I want to dedicate this chapter to not just the four friends I mentioned, but also to those friends who have come and gone in my journey. Too many to name, you know who you are. Thank you for the seasons you were a part of my life. I learned so much about myself and from you as well during those seasons. Thank you to the ones I still connect with from time to time. Knowing you are still there for me is a blessing.

Thank you to the new friends I have made throughout my journey. Thank you for sticking around so far. I'm looking forward to the life lessons and wisdom I will gain from each and every one of you. Now in my late 30s (38 to be exact) I have come to a place in my life where I have accepted the loss of friendships and there have been quite a few. Before, when I was younger, it would bug me when friends would come and go. I didn't understand it's a part of life. I thought it was my fault, something was wrong with me. I would do anything to try to keep my friendships close.

I am constantly learning boundaries in my friendships. The lesson I have learned is, some are meant to be in our journey for a season and some are what I like to call "Lifers". My riders till the end. Some of the friends I thought would be lifers are no longer a part of my journey. There are many seasons we will go through in our lives, but we are not alone. He is with us and will bring the people to help us in our journeys.

I wanna say Thank you! from the bottom of my heart! Thank you for being who you are in my life. You're blessings and gifts from God. Thank you for never giving up on me, for uplifting, correcting, for challenging, for teaching me how to be a true friend. For accepting me with quirks, faults, mistakes and all. I'm forever grateful! Love you con todo mi corazón.

Your friend,
Merami

CHAPTER 8
M.C. Days

"Just because you fail once, doesn't mean you're gonna
fail at everything!"
Marilyn Monroe

I was introduced to a discipleship program, Masters Commission. The group who I was first introduced to was located in Manteca back then and they came to the church I grew up in, Ebenezer in Sacramento. Masters Commission was and still is a school of discipleship and ministry. The one I was most familiar with was located in Manteca California. Looking back at it now, why didn't I just go to that one? Oh I know why.... I wanted to leave Sacramento. I was looking for a new experience, something more than what I was so used to experiencing at the church I grew up in, Ebenezer Christian Center, now known as The Avenue Church.

Trying to find an escape from being in Sacramento, I went online and checked out the Masters Commission website. I found out by research that there was one in the city of Marysville. I thought, "cool", Marysville, CA. Nope!- I was wrong, it was Marysville, WA. For me it was even better. I get to leave Sacramento, forget that, I get to leave California! I went to the website where the Masters Commission was located. Marysville Masters Commission. It was the Drama Ministry that caught my eye. I filled out an information card online thinking oh they won't send me anything. To my surprise, they did. I was sent an application and even received a phone call several days later. I was 18 years old, had just graduated high school and I wanted to explore more but not in Sacramento, so Washington was the perfect choice. At least that's what I thought.

The MC program started in October of 2002. But I couldn't start in October. I didn't have the finances to pay the deposit and my parents didn't either. I was able to arrive later that same school year. I ended up moving to Marysville Washington in January 2003. Before leaving Sacramento I had spent what I thought at that time would be my last Christmas and New Years with my family. I didn't know when I would see them again. Masters Commission is a 4 year program. I was so certain that I would be there for 4 years. I was mistaken! I was in the program for only 18 months. I didn't know then that my leaving would hurt my relationship with my siblings. It has taken a lot to repair the hurt I put them through. We all haven't sat down to talk about it. Being the youngest of 4, they didn't like the idea of me leaving.

My oldest brother was very supportive. He thought it would teach me responsibility and I would mature. I like to say I did to an extent. If anything, I became more aware of how I'm treated and have been able to stand up for myself and not tolerate any kind of abuse, well sort of. My twin sister, on the other hand, was not used to not having me around (except for that year and a half). I was always with her. So that was hard for her to accept not having me, her partner in crime. It was hard on both of us. With me being in WA, we would spend one birthday apart and not together. Our last year in our teens and I would be many miles away and not with her.

Since then I have always wanted to spend our birthday together. I feel like I owe her that. Now, we try to spend every birthday together. My 2nd older brother, who was also married for a few years at the time I didn't know how he felt and I never talked to him about it. There are still some conversations we haven't had to this day. We've never talked about my time in WA. My siblings were living their own lives and I felt like it was time for me to find mine and live it. I wanted to prove to them that I was not the younger sibling who was spoiled but was all grown up and who could make her own decisions. I even failed at that -proving to them I could do it on my own.

It was a hard hit for my family when I left. It was also a hard hit for my parents not just financially but emotionally. My parents did so much for me before I left. My mom, bless her beautiful heart, made dozens of tamales to sell just for me to pay the deposit of $1000 plus more for me to get into Marysville Masters Commission Program. I don't remember how much the full cost of the program was for. I just know it was a lot on them. It was definitely a struggle for them financially.

All I remember is that my parents ended up paying a lot of money and for what? For me to fail the program and get kicked out. One of the biggest failures I have experienced in my life. Why did I fail? I wasn't treated fairly and I stood up for myself to one of the leaders and that was not a pleasant sight. I got in her face and told her off and disrespected her in front of staff and my classmates. I forgot to mention that my mom was not at peace with me leaving. She didn't know how to show her feelings towards me leaving, so she didn't say much to me even at the airport the day I left. She hugged me with tears in her eyes, no words but those tears said a lot to me! Her tearful eyes told me "I love you mijita. Don't leave, you're not yet ready to face the world." But all I felt was a drive to leave and be on my own. Not realizing that I would have a bad experience and it would be hard to get back on my feet afterwards because I felt embarrassed and ashamed for being kicked out of the program.

My dad came with me to drop me off to the Masters Commission Program. We flew from Sacramento,CA to Seattle, WA. About an hour away from Marysville, the city I lived in while I was in the program. My new roommate picked us up from the airport and took us to what would be my new house for the time I would be in the program. In the Masters Commission program you were placed in the houses of the church members that would open their homes to the students. We called them home openers. In my first year, the house I lived in was the Merrit Family's house. My new roommate and I were to stay there for the year we would be in the Masters Commission Program. My Roommate (who will only be referred to as my Roommate to protect privacy) was a 2nd year student, while I was a new 1st year student. During the time we lived in the house, we had to do chores and make sure our part of the house was kept nice and clean. I will admit, I had never done house chores growing up, my mom did all the cleaning for us when we lived in Texas. When we moved to Sacramento, I don't recall when living with our aunt that we did chores. I remember cleaning the church on Saturdays at the age of 5 years old, when we lived in Texas but not doing chores at home. I was so green when I arrived at the M.C. Program. I had to learn to clean, and also do my own laundry. Thanks to my Roommate, because she taught me how.

I had to get used to the fact that I was no longer in CA. I was the odd one of the bunch. I didn't look like the staff or students, all preppy, skinny, and White. I was the dark one there which is odd because my skin is fair like ivory fair. I felt different from everyone else. I felt like I didn't belong. I was a different shade of white to them. I was the only female Hispanic there. To make matters worse, I was overweight. I was at my heaviest then, 220 pounds, and it was the main factor they (the leadership) used to manipulate and take advantage of me. I was bullied because of my weight and because I was different. I looked different, spoke differently and thought differently. My differences made me a target as well as a threat. It didn't help much that I had arrived later than everyone else. Everyone started the program in October and I joined the program in January. Cliques and groups were already made. The first years students were with the first years, second years students with the second years, and the third years students were staff, the upper class of the school presumed all the responsibilities of the Masters Commission.

Some second year students were able to have leadership roles. First years were not. It was stricter for the first year students. First years could not have a job or be in a romantic relationship. First years had to focus on school and ministry. There could be no distractions. I was not only from California, but I was a Hispanic from California. The students thought that since I was from California, I knew how to surf. and I was stereotyped because of it. I was from NorCal, not SoCal. There's a big difference between the two. I also had a mixed Texan and Californian accent. So even the way I talked, or explained things was odd to them.

My first day of school for the Masters Commission program was odd. I'd figured we would be in one of the classrooms of the church where the school was being held. The school program was located on the bottom part of the church. We called it the dungeon. Yep! It was a dungeon. It had a main room where we met every morning for prayer and devotions. There were also classrooms and restrooms in the building. The classrooms were like a class setting with tables and desks. I must admit, I sometimes felt like we were trapped there for days. We did everything that had to do with the MC program in that dungeon. That was our MC campus. On my first day, I walked into a room (dungeon) full of students and were all in a circle holding hands and praying in tongues. Something I was not so used to seeing let alone praying. It was loud and sounded like when you make a gun sound with your mouth. I was thrown off by it. I was not used to that kind of scene. I thought you prayed in tongues when the Spirit moved in you. This looked like it was rehearsed. When I joined the circle, I felt odd because I wasn't speaking in tongues. I had my eyes closed tightly as I prayed. Then I said to myself, join them, you can speak in tongues too. Speak. So I did. I spoke in tongues, I didn't want to be left out. We ended the prayer and it was time for devotionals and bible memory verse study. Afterwards, we had to attend our scheduled classes. My dad was still with me. He was in the room during the prayer session we just had. After the prayer, I gave him a big hug and told him "okay Dad, I am here now, you have nothing to worry about. You can go home." I was trying to be brave at that moment. I didn't want my dad to see that I was scared. He was also brave, he didn't show emotion but I know he cried on his way home. My dad lets his emotions out when he's by himself. He rarely says much but when he does, you better listen.

My Dad didn't leave until he spoke with the school director. I don't know what they talked about. I'd figured they talked about the program and what his little girl was going to be doing in the program. They talked about home situations, and he paid the deposit. My Dad left. I was all alone in a place I didn't know. With people I didn't know who later would be a big part of my journey. Some that to this day have been in my life and some who I have forgotten and have had let go. It was a scary feeling being left alone without my parents or my family by my side. I may have been smiling on the outside, but on the inside, I was screaming for help. I was terrified. I wasn't ready for the change, and the new life I was going to embark on.

My major of study for the program was Drama Ministry with a minor in Youth Ministry. I also participated on the Worship team for many of the outreaches we were invited to minister at. I also volunteered at youth church services. I helped out in the youth conferences as a chaperone and cabin leader at the youth camps. Now before I go more in depth about my experience in the Masters Commission Program, I got permission from one of my former classmates to be mentioned in this chapter. Rachel. You'll see why I decided to mention her. For the sake of privacy, we will call the other individual Bri. They both played a big role in this part of my journey. They too experienced something similar to what I did sometime after I was kicked out of the MC program. It was on my second day being there, I didn't know anyone there so I stayed close by my Roommate for the first couple of days of the program. We both had our own ministry internships to attend after we had our Bible College courses for the day. My Roommate was a youth leader, so she would meet in the Youth chapel for her internship. She also taught piano lessons twice a week to the younger students from the youth group.

I remember meeting The Drama Ministry Leader in the Drama room. She is from Alaska and when she mentioned it to me, right away my mind thought she must be an Eskimo. I stereotyped her thinking she lived in an igloo and fished for a living. I was wrong in my childish thinking. I have never been to Alaska but just by looking at some pictures, it's a beautiful sight that I hope one day to see. I felt like I was the odd one, the different one. I was told by the leadership I was too big for certain plays and they did everything they could to make sure I was not " too big for ministry". They'd used the verse that talks about "your body is a temple" to make me feel like I was wrong in being overweight. I am Latina, I am supposed to be curvy! To them, I was too curvy. They were not used to having a petite overweight student. Not to mention a Latina student.

It was so hard for me even during the outreaches, I couldn't eat what everyone else ate, I was told to eat more salads, and not too many carbs. It was unfair. No one else had to do the dieting but me. Looking back at it, I would call it abuse. I was angry, confused, and felt like I was too small and the leadership were giants. I felt helpless and hopeless. I couldn't defeat them. The giants that haunted me and made me feel like I would lose the fight if I were to fight them.

That was not the only big issue. I had a hard time getting along with The Drama Ministry Leader. It wasn't my weight that made it difficult to work with each other, it was my attitude. Bratty attitude if I may add. I took all my anger, my frustration that I had with the main leadership on her. Also, I was jealous of her popularity with everyone else. She could get along with everyone but me. I wanted to be her friend. But our clashes didn't help. We could not see eye to eye. We just could not get along or work together. She had expectations as the leader to have everything perfect and she would be upset with me for not getting the steps and the acting part like she wanted me to and that made things worse. It didn't help either one of us, me with my attitude, and her with her high expectations and perfectionism. It was an ongoing frustrating situation. Neither of us had imagined that our issues would ever be resolved and we could eventually get along and work well together.

I can now say, The Drama Ministry Leader and I are friends. We stayed in touch over the years after she decided to leave the Masters Commission Program. I reached out to her to bury the hatchet and she was pleasantly surprised that I reached out to her on one of her birthdays through Facebook. I found out later while talking to her about what really happened, why we really clashed, it was all because she had so much pressure from the leadership. She had a standard she was expected to meet. The leadership wanted her to help me be more involved in a leadership role during my 2nd school year and to give me more responsibility. They wanted me to help her with the props and the drama equipment. Not only that, the leadership wanted her to mistreat me to see how much I could take, and if I would decide to quit or get kicked out of the program.

The Drama Ministry was the main reason why I enrolled into the MC program. I wanted to learn more about the Drama Ministry. The thought of acting to a song, and playing characters and telling a story of the Gospel of Jesus fascinated me! That is what drew me to the Masters Commission Program when I first saw it at my home church in Sacramento. But I was not sure I wanted the leadership role at the time, I just wanted to fix the clash that hindered The Drama Ministry Leader and I from getting along and working together. I acted out and lashed out at her because I wasn't being heard. I was ignored and was told that it was too much for me to try to fix the issue. It was pointless to them. Later on while being in the MC Program I apologized to her but I was still angry with her because we still clashed. I felt like she hated me. I was not used to that, because I felt like I was liked by everyone else there. I didn't know what it meant to truly submit and not argue back and be on the defensive side with leadership.

She recently told me her intention was never to make me feel the way I felt. She didn't know how to be a help to me, because she was told by the director to take me under her wing and mentor me. He was in charge, and what he'd say would go, whether you agree with him or not! The director manipulated not just the students, but the leaders under him as well.

I still remember one time, we were in the drama room. I couldn't get the steps down for a skit we would be doing for the outreach that weekend. The skit was to the song, "The Change" by Steven Curtis Chapman. I am Latina, but I was not used to these kinds of steps. I was used to Cumbia dance moves, so these steps were a challenge for me. These steps were more a mixture of step and ballet. I was not used to those steps. I didn't get the steps, and my acting portrayal of the song was not too convincing, and the leadership was there watching as well. I got so nervous. I tend to get nervous when I am being watched, I tense up or even cowardly put my head down to not look at anyone.

I remember that day I yelled at the Drama Ministry Leader and left the room because, one, I was embarrassed. It takes a lot to get me to that point. Secondly, I stood up for myself and I wanted to show everyone there, you don't mess with me or treat me that way. I left the room shaking and felt like I wanted to throw up. That's what usually happens, I get that feeling when I get really scared or really angry.

I didn't know that on that day when I yelled at The Drama Ministry leader she was given some bad news that a family member of hers had passed away. She had to leave on an emergency trip to Alaska to be with family. I found this out recently when she and I talked about our experience in the MC program. I also don't know why no one in leadership tried to inform me during the time it happened. But they thought it would be a great idea for me to join a few of our classmates to pick up The Drama Ministry Leader from the airport. That night is still a bit vague and fuzzy. I can only remember going to the airport to pick her up and then going to eat an early breakfast at a restaurant. The rest of that night is blocked from my memory.

Drama rehearsals while I was there were difficult for me. I dreaded it each time. I didn't have emotional sentiment for the role in the skit I performed in. The way they treated me made me feel like a "big fat failure". The taste of failure was nauseating. I hated it, and I hated myself for failing. I questioned my ability to even succeed in the program. My first year did not go the way I'd expected it to go.

During my 1st year in the MC program, I dealt with so much depression, anxiety, even thoughts of suicide because I didn't feel like I belonged. I also had a bad break up with J.D. my first boyfriend. He cheated on me when I was away. My world was turned upside down. Too many emotions built up and I ate my feelings. I sneaky-snacked at night and became an emotional eater. I was a hot mess! To top all that, my bubbly side was outcasted, rejected and looked down upon. I had to learn to "fit in", in a place where I felt like I wasn't even wanted. I was looked at as a burden. I was not accepted. I looked for the acceptance of the leadership and I didn't get it. I felt like I made the biggest mistake in my life joining the program. I hated being there and also hated myself for leaving Sacramento the one place I was so familiar with. Washington became the place that stretched me to my limit and it broke me.

The bible classes were a different story. I felt like maybe I could succeed there with my studies. I did all I could to get good grades. I was good at remembering Bible verses. I was a bible nerd. I still am today. In my first year, I passed my classes. That was the only good thing I had going for me. My studies. The professor, a precious sweet man who I still talk to today, he would not teach too much, our class would turn into a church service. Singing, preaching and then an altar call. While he preached and sang, the students would work on the assignments and the homework. I passed his class with flying colors. I had so much happening my first year. Traveling every weekend, ministering at the outreaches, hardly eating after the outreaches, stressed out, papers due, class assignments, church events, and home chores. At 19 it was a lot on my body that I would binge eat when I was not at school or had anyone watching that it would get back to the director or the staff. I actually got sick a couple of times because of all the stress and pressure I was under.

In Spring of my first year, my Roommate and I were in a bad car accident. We were on our way to the Director's house for a BBQ and some sports activities. We were moments away from arriving at a complete stop and about to make a left turn, when we were rear ended by a car behind us who was going 40 mph before making a complete stop. I was so scared I blacked out. We both had some bad injuries. I injured my lower back and shoulder. I also got whiplashed from hitting my head on the dashboard (something I do not recall). My Roommate injured her neck and back as well. We had to go through chiropractic therapy for a couple of years to heal from our injuries. We ended up going to the BBQ that night, all sore from the accident. We told the staff what happened and they seemed concerned but not really. We were told that we both still had to attend our outreach that night. It was Evangelism night. No exceptions! No excuses, we had to be there! Both my Roommate and I didn't have a vehicle or any other kind of transportation to meet at the church for the event. None of the students or staff were willing or able to pick us up. I personally didn't want to go. We had just gotten into a bad car accident and I was in so much pain. Despite our excruciating pain, my Roommate and I walked to the church; we walked from the house where we stayed to the church. I'd say it was about 2.5 miles, maybe even more. It was a long walk!

Later that night of the accident, my twin sister called me frantically on the phone. Since we are twins, we both have something called twin telepathy. She knew something had happened to me. I didn't call anyone back home when I had the accident. My twin sister felt pain on her lower back and her shoulder and she knew to call me to make sure I was okay. When she called, I told her about the accident and then a couple of moments later, my mom called me to see if I was okay. I told my mom to not worry, my Roommate will look into getting this taken care of and her insurance should cover most of the expenses. I was wrong, it was a long road to recovery for me as well as getting a lawyer to help us with the case.

I came home during Spring break of 2003 to visit after being in the MC Program for 4 months. One of the staff members wanted to join me on my visit back home. She was sent by the director to join me to keep an eye on me. I know that now. Even in my own home, being with my family, I felt like I was walking on eggshells. I felt like a prisoner. I couldn't be my true self. I had changed. I didn't feel like I had made the right choice of going into the MC Program. I played it off because I didn't want anyone in my family to think I had made a huge mistake in going into the MC program. My mom noticed it. She knew something was wrong. She tried to talk to me about it, but I didn't tell her the whole truth. I just told her it was taking me time to get used to the change. I didn't want her to know what I was being put through, how I was being treated.

My parents and family to this day don't know everything I went through. All they know is that I was dismissed (kicked out) of the program. They don't know that I trashed the motorhome I lived in during my 2nd year. I was so angry with the leadership of the MC program, I wanted to prove to them and to myself that I was not going to be treated the way they treated me. I kept it to myself and then I exploded when I trashed the motorhome. I've only done that once in my lifetime.

The Saturday before I was kicked out, the home opener was cleaning their house and had asked me to help out. Since I was not feeling well, I ignored her and went inside the motorhome and played music to rest. Well, she called the director and told him what I did and on the following Monday morning, I was told I had a week to pack my belongings and leave the program. I was told I was too much to handle. I was not a good fit for the program. I was dismissed for "bad behavior".

Let me back up a bit. I graduated my 1st year from the program but my family could not make it to the ceremony. It was so hard for me to celebrate alone. I missed my family, I was sad that they could not attend. Me graduating, that itself was a big accomplishment to me because I survived a year of bad treatment, emotional stress, anxiety, overeating, suicidal thoughts, and depression. Not to mention, my dad's health was getting worse. During my first year in the MC program, he had to get eye surgery on top of other health complications. During that time, things between the Drama Ministry Leader and I were still yet to be resolved. I made it a mission to return to my 2nd year to fix the issue. I felt like since I made the mess, I had to clean it up and patch things up.

Going back for my 2nd year was not easy. I was given an ultimatum. I was told if I wanted to return to my 2nd year, I had to lose 20lbs, and find a job during the summer break. I lost 15lbs and did get a job that summer. I was accepted to return as a 2nd year student. I was ready for a new year. A better experience. To my surprise it didn't go well. It was worse than my first year. My 2nd year there, I was moved from one home opener to another. They couldn't find a place for the "brown fat girl". While the leadership looked for a home for me to stay in, I stayed at the parent's home of one of the staff members. I stayed there for 2 days.

The leadership found a place for me to stay. I wasn't even placed in an actual home. I was left outside in the cold in a motorhome. Not one but 2 of them to be exact. The first motorhome was a bit further from the school and since I didn't have a car they moved me closer to the school. The second motorhome I lived in was small. The family I lived with had stuffed dead animal heads inside their home, you can smell the animals. Their house was carpeted with checkered red and black colors like a flannel shirt a fisherman wears. They had two daughters ages 4 and 6. I don't remember their names or the home opener's names. I just remember their home. It felt like I was on a country reality show. I lived there in the cold winter of Marysville WA. It is not just any normal California cold weather, it's much more brutal than that. Snowy, icy, winter. Did I mention my roommate at the time loved to run at 5am in the cold winter and would have me tag along?

The 2nd motorhome, which was the last one I stayed in, my roommate Rachel and I, lived there. We tried to make it work. We got along really well. I still talk to her today. We kept in touch over the years with the help of social media. Facebook has been our connection. Rachel was my last roommate in the MC program. She wanted to live with me. She practically begged and pleaded with the staff to allow her to live with me. I met her my first year, a couple of days after I arrived at the program. Rachel is not very vocal, but she has a sweet personality. When we both were first year students, she helped me with catching up with my classes and always made sure I was on track with our crazy schedule. We always studied at a grocery store with a restaurant inside, Haggens. That was our spot to eat and study. We sometimes were there late at night studying for tests and working on homework. We also went to Cristianos Italian restaurant for lunch breaks. One chicken alfredo plate can feed three people. So yummy and the Cesar salad was so good too. I discovered my love for pasta and bread when I was in the MC program. I still love bread and pasta but don't always eat it, unless I go to Olive Garden.

I learned a lot being in the MC program, not just about myself but about those around me. I learned to cook, clean, and learned what behind the scenes of ministry was like. I also learned how to read people, and what their true intentions are. I learned to not be so naive and let people step on me. I learned that I am a meek person and it has sometimes been seen as a weakness. Even today, people see me as a super nice, innocent person, they don't know what I have been through in my early years as a Worship Leader or my journey in Ministry. They don't know how much of a fight I fought. At one point in my life during my time in the MC Program, I almost gave up completely! I was so done with everything and everyone! I was also home sick. I wanted out. I felt like I was a big failure and God didn't love me for failing. I would read the Bible and I was dead inside. No emotion, emptiness, depression, guilt and shame tried to knock me down so low that I couldn't, and wouldn't get up.

Rachel saw me in the emotional, spiritual state I was in. I don't remember what we were talking about exactly one night but she got so mad at me and threw the Bible at me and with passion and holy anger she told me "Either you believe this book, or you don't! God's word is true! It's time for you to get up and believe it and remember who you are and whose you are! You're a child of God!" I'll never forget that come-to-grips moment in the motorhome Rachel and I both lived in. She not only called me out on my disbelief but challenged me to decide what I believed in. She believed in the greatness I carried and didn't want to see me give up or stay defeated. I thank God for that night. I thank God for Rachel.

So what drove me to trash the motorhome? I was so mad at myself, mad at the world, and I had anger issues. I exposed them that day I trashed the motorhome. I unleashed everything I had inside. All the anger, the resentment, the self hate, the heart ache, I took it out on the motorhome. I left it dirty, hangers and clothes everywhere and broken mirrors. Glass on the floor left it all there for someone else to clean it up. At that point, I didn't care! That was my revenge- in a way I was telling the MC program to... well you know what I mean. You can finish the sentence in your head. I wasn't able to get all my belongings after leaving. The leadership decided to keep it as collateral since the home openers didn't press any charges for me destroying their property. I'm not proud of what I did. I still can't believe it got to that point, but it did! I had reached a breaking point!

I came back home on December 26, 2003. The night before Christmas Day, I spent it with my first year Roommate and a couple of friends who were in the MC program drinking alcohol, watching movies and playing card games. A night I'll never forget because that night I didn't care what I did, I stopped myself because the way I was behaving wasn't me. I was depressed, mad, and felt so much shame because I failed. I was kicked out of The MC program. How can I go home? On my flight home on December 26, 2003, I kept thinking to myself, how am I gonna explain the truth to my parents, to my friends, to the church? What am I gonna say? I cried on my flight home. My flight landed in Sacramento California that evening of December 26, 2003. My twin sister, and her boyfriend at the time, who is now her husband, my brother-in-law accompanied her to pick me up.

On the night before I flew home, I talked to my mom and sister on the phone and my mom begged me to come home and forget about my studies because my dad wasn't doing well. My mom didn't tell me what was really going on with my dad. All she told me was to come home.

My family had kept it from me that my dad had foot surgery because he had broken his foot. I thought my sister would take me to our house. Instead she took me to the hospital to see my dad. That was the first stop after my flight home. Suddenly, being home didn't feel like I had thought it would feel. I felt worried, anxious and fearful for my dad. We arrived at the hospital and I felt so anxious like I was going to throw up. I was scared to see my dad in the hospital bed with this round thing around his foot and pins and needles on it. I gave him a hug and asked him what happened? "He said I am okay Miija don't worry. I'm glad you're home". My Superman, my hero was in the hospital and I didn't like it. He's supposed to be strong and nothing can break him. Nothing can hold him down and keep him on a hospital bed. He had that halo on his foot for about 6 weeks after being in the hospital for a couple of days.

I was home and things changed. I changed. I wasn't me. I was so bitter and full of guilt and shame. I was always angry. I hated the person I had become. I would go to church feeling guilty that when I was asked how come I returned home, I said I missed my family and needed to be here with them and because my dad was in the hospital. Deep down inside I knew that wasn't the whole truth.

That same Summer, after going home, the staff and students from the Marysville MC Program decided to come to Sacramento on their way home from their annual Mexico/Camping trip. I honestly didn't want to see them. I didn't want to see them because I would be reminded of the failure I was and how I was kicked out of the program. Little did I know that the truth would come out when they met with my Senior Pastor and Youth Pastor at my Sacramento Church and told them what I had done and why I left the program. I was asked by my youth pastor to meet with him before church on a Wednesday night. He wanted to talk to me.

 I didn't expect to have the director of the MC Program and his assistant to be in the room waiting for me. They told my senior and youth pastor the whole truth about why I was kicked out of the program. With my head down and tears in my eyes, I came clean. I told my pastors the truth. I told them about my constant disagreements with The Drama Ministry Leader. The truth was finally out. I didn't leave MC, I was kicked out! They were shocked and disappointed in me. The Senior Pastor later after the meeting placed me in discipline. I was okay with that because I didn't want anything to do with ministry. I was done! I had thrown in the towel. I gave up. I didn't want to get up. It was too embarrassing for me to get up because I had to face the reality that I was kicked out of the MC Program for bad behavior. I was not known to be like that. My testimony was tarnished.

During the time I was in discipline, I wept at every altar call. I brought so much shame to myself and to my church so I thought that I needed to be forgiven, but I was already forgiven, I just hadn't forgiven myself. I held on to that shame for a long time. Looking back now, I wallowed in self-pity and self unforgiveness. I was too ashamed to get up, to even step on a stage and sing on a worship team.

Despite all that, I still got up! It was hard and painful but I got back up! I kept fighting. And I am still fighting! I thank God for the experiences and the lessons I learned during that season of my life. I wouldn't be where I am today if I had not gotten kicked out of the MC Program. I wouldn't be the strong woman I am today. I wouldn't have learned to submit to my leadership. I wouldn't have learned what ministry can be like behind the scenes. I wouldn't have learned to trust God and rebuild my relationship with Him.

I may have failed, but that didn't and doesn't define me. I may have wanted to give up and never get up. But I didn't give up! I got up!! And you can too! It doesn't matter what you have done in your past, what matters is what you do after you have failed. God cares about you and does not hold your past against you or remembers your past, He still loves you and will use you if you let Him. Give Him all your cares, because He does care about you! He wants His best for your life!

CHAPTER 9
Identity Crisis

"If I can't sing, then who am I?"
-Merami-

On April 4, 2012, I woke up with what I thought was a bad sore throat. I couldn't make any sound. I couldn't speak, it was too painful. I couldn't swallow or drink anything. This pain was so excruciating all I could do was cry. Crying made it worse. Anything I did made it worse. I was so scared. What happened to my voice? I lost it! The diagnosis, laryngitis. The way I can describe the painful feeling is having someone go inside your throat and scrape it with the sharpest knife over and over and you can't make a sound to make it stop. I didn't just experience this one time, but twice in a period of less than 6 months that year. I lost my voice. The essence of who I was was gone. I was nobody without my voice. That's what I thought. It was a painful experience all around. I didn't just lose my voice, in a way I lost myself. I didn't know who I was without my voice. That's what I was known for, singing, leading on Sundays and the fact that I could no longer sing crushed me. I dealt with an identity crisis. I didn't know who I was. From April 2012-December 2012, was a season in my journey where I had to rediscover my identity in God. It was the season where I lost my voice twice because of laryngitis. A season of so much fear and doubt, I lost myself in the process of it. I didn't know who I was. I didn't have a voice, I couldn't sing, or talk. I felt hopeless. I felt like I was done and I would never sing again. The fear of not knowing what I would sound like after I recuperated was daunting.

Before I lost my voice, I was not properly taking care of my voice. I was drinking coffee and soda like it was water. I would not warm up my voice before leading at the events where I led worship. I was also traveling every weekend with Double Portion, the worship band that I was a part of at the time. I would use my throat more than sing from my diaphragm. My breathing technique was not properly used. Double Portion was a part of many 24-48 hour Worship events where Worship Teams were invited to lead the prayer services all over California and other States as well. At each of these events we would sing for about 5 hours on the weekend.

Back then, I didn't rest when I needed to. I would be so exhausted after traveling and I had to be at church to lead on Sunday mornings with hoarseness and excruciating pain in my throat. I didn't know the damage I was putting my throat through. I was damaging my instrument and I didn't know it. I may have been in pain, but that didn't stop me. I enjoyed the rush and the adrenaline I felt. God was using me in my gift. I was "being obedient" to the call God placed on my life. I enjoyed being a part of something big that was happening in California. However, I was in excruciating pain, and I still sang on those weekends. Bad idea! I don't recommend it. When your body tells you to take a break, you better listen. Also I recommend vocal warm ups if you're going to be singing/ leading for an event. You want to make sure your voice is properly cared for. I had to learn the hard way. All that soda, coffee, fried foods, and spicy foods along with lack of rest damaged my throat. I know better now!

Being a part of Double Portion, opened a couple of doors for us. We got to minister alongside some of the greatest Worship leaders in the country like Rick Pino, Leland, Jenn Johnson, Eddie James, and Catherine Mullins to name a few. I even met Rick Pino & Jenn Johnson in our green room and took a photo with them and got to talk to them a bit about worship. The Call Sacramento was the event where I met them. A couple of years ago, Catherine Mullins and I reconnected over social media and still talk today. We message each other and check in with each other frequently. I'm blessed to call her a friend and sister in Christ. She was there for me when I was in a transition period in my life. She prayed and encouraged me through it.

The Call Sacramento was a 3 Day event Thursday-Saturday. It was in the hot summer of 2010. It was before all the weekend traveling began. In fact that gave Double Portion the launch to be invited to many Worship Conferences and Prayer Gatherings. The Call was the first big event we ministered at. It was a great turnout. So many people gathered together at Raley Field in Sacramento California. We were all so excited and nervous about the event but we pulled through. We ended that first night with a bang and the next morning all over again until that evening, and on the last day we closed the event . It was packed and God did something in Sacramento that weekend. You can see for yourself, our worship set is on YouTube. That was my life. Traveling every weekend. I'd get home early the next morning with sometimes 2-3 hours of sleep because I wouldn't go to bed right away when I'd get home, I would stay up trying to wind down from the adrenaline and the coffee I had during the event. I did that non stop for a period of almost 3 years.

The morning of April 4, 2012 was the beginning of one of the hardest moments in my life. I needed to know what was going on with my throat. The first thing I did was go to Urgent Care and was given a steroid to clear the infection. I had to get more than one steroid and that still didn't fix the issue. Finding the solution took months. Months of tests, of trying to figure out what was wrong with my throat, left me in a state of feeling I was no one without my voice. I was even told by a doctor that if I ever want to sing or talk again, I need to take a break. Those words were hard to hear. I didn't want a break. I was the one who was always there ready to sing and to lead. I didn't say No. Another lesson I had to learn during that season. I now know, it's okay to say "No" when you can't go on, and you don't have to feel bad for saying No!

The steroids didn't help much so I had to go to an ENT doctor to get a flexible laryngoscopy done. That's when the flexible laryngoscope is inserted into the patient's nose, moved into the throat and positioned near the affected area. During the procedure, the patient may feel a strange sensation of the scope through the nose, however he or she will be able to breathe normally. I was so scared thinking my vocal chords were damaged. Thank God that was not the case!

So what was causing the laryngitis and the excruciating pain? I thought it was nodules on my vocal chords. Nodules are polyps inside your throat that are not only painful but can keep growing and will need to be surgically removed. That was not the case for me either, thank God!

The diagnosis was acid reflux and a minor case of sleep apnea. What??? Acid reflux??? Yes! Heartburn is what was causing me to have pain in my throat. I had to change my diet. I had to stop eating greasy food and spicy food. I also gave up coffee. That was hard to do because I love coffee. I couldn't have my go-to drink from Starbucks coffee; an iced white mocha. Those were some sad days.

I still drink coffee today but not like I used to. I'll splurge here and there but not excessively. The Ear Nose & Throat Specialist (ENT) also recommended that I get a sleep test done. He mentioned it because I snore at night, that too is causing the pain and irritation at night. The specialists scheduled me for a sleep apnea test. I wasn't able to get it done because my medical insurance had lapsed and it would be too expensive out of pocket. However, I still wanted to get it done; It seemed like a fun experience. For the sleep apnea test, you're sent to a sleep lab that looks like a hotel and you have the whole room to yourself, filled with snacks but no water. The downfall is that before the test, you have to be awake for 24 hours. During this test, you're hooked up to equipment that monitors your heart, lung and brain activity, breathing patterns, arm and leg movements, and blood oxygen levels while you sleep. I still have to get that test done today.

My recovery season was intense. I felt like Rocky Balboa, in the fifth film from the movie franchise where he lost it all and he had to retire because he had gotten brain damage. That's how I felt! I felt like I lost everything and I didn't know if I would get it back. I felt weird not being able to do what I love to do which is sing and lead worship. If I wasn't up there on the platform singing, I felt like I was irrelevant, I was a nobody, like I was forgotten. It was a scary feeling of not knowing if you're going to sound the same after recovering from losing your voice. I was afraid to sing. I didn't sing during that time. I barely spoke. I was quiet. It was odd even to my friends and family that I couldn't talk. I was always singing and talking before I lost my voice. Being a people person. I enjoy great conversations. I love to sing, I like to share my thoughts with those around me in my circle. So when I couldn't do that, I freaked out. Who was I without my voice, without singing and leading Sunday morning at church? I was just me. I felt useless. That's all I knew. That's what I was known for. My voice.

During my recovery, I missed being up on the platform, singing, and leading. I missed it. I would go to church and it was hard to see everyone else do what I was called to do. It was so hard to face my reality not knowing when I would be able to sing or step on the platform again. My heart ached for it. I wanted to be up there and a couple of times God spoke to me telling me it was necessary. The break I had to forcefully take was necessary. I now understand that it was. Back then, I didn't understand and it was hard for me to accept. It was necessary for me to realize who I sang for. Was this for my fame or His fame? I had to realize the reason why I sang. Those 8 months were difficult yet at the same time very teachable. I learned a lot about myself and God's Grace. I threw many pity parties and cried so much but His Grace, and His Love held me up and kept me faithful to Him and I learned to accept the season I was in at that time.

It wasn't easy, I fought every day believing in God's Word and His promises for my life. I would even try to sing little by little and I didn't like my voice. I didn't like the rasp I had developed and the softness of the sound of my voice. It didn't sound like me. I wasn't used to the new sound coming from my voice. I questioned it.

These were my thoughts, "this isn't me". "I don't sound like this". "Why do I sound like this?" "What happened to my high pitch, why am I only able to sing in alto range. I sound like a man. I don't like this!!! I couldn't sing soprano! I was an alto. It took a while for me to get used to the sound of my voice. I had to learn to not just accept my voice but love the sound and the new range and ranges it developed during that time.

Something I still struggle with today. I sometimes don't like my voice but I have learned to trust God with my instrument. I have to remind myself about this journey. The season I lost my voice, I didn't know what that experience would teach me. In retrospect, It taught me that it has and will never be about me. I am just His vessel. If I am willing and have the right motives, He will use me.

I share this because I don't just want to share my story, my prayer is for you, the reader, to know you're not alone in this journey. We all in one way or another have felt lost in ourselves, in our own journeys, our own paths. We even have felt alone or that no one understands what we feel or go through. That is not true. In my journey, I have come to find out that when I am going through something or have gone through something, someone else has already experienced what I went through or is going through it at the same time as me. It may even look different because all our journeys are distinct but we can relate to one another. We can share the lessons we learned and how we overcame our life experiences. We are not alone! We may feel lonely, but we are not alone. Yes sometimes we need to face things by ourselves because we are best equipped for it and ultimately we can come out of the situation stronger and wiser.

The time we spend with ourselves is not only crucial but necessary. To sit down and quiet all the noise around us and just be alone with God is so needed. We need that time to get to know ourselves. Who are we really? Can we be raw with Jesus and ourselves? Can we take off the mask and speak truthfully and openly?

When I was able to sing again after my recovery season, (since I didn't like my voice) I struggled with accepting my sound. I even tried to mimic other singers. I tried to lead worship like them. I questioned my ability to sing, to lead worship. If I didn't sound like them, I wasn't "good enough or anointed". God spoke to me and told me I'm not like everyone else. I wasn't created to be a copy of someone else. God grabbed my attention a lot during that season in the most loving fatherly way. He reminded me that I have a purpose. That He's not done with me yet. I don't need to understand but trust in Him and let His Spirit guide me and lead my every step of this journey.

Going through this season almost destroyed me spiritually. I lost myself. I lost the spark, the light I carried had dimmed. I dealt with questioning my sense of self. I let the doubt and fear of what I was facing control me. I also dealt with depression. I was so sad because I couldn't sing anymore. I was angry at God. I blamed Him and questioned His will for my life. I threw many tantrums and I didn't like that season. I hated the fact that I may never sing again or sound like me again. The thought of me being "no one" without singing again or leading worship haunted me. That's all I knew to do. So I thought. I had forgotten about my other passion to study God's word and preach. Singing, it was a big part of me. People would say, "oh you know Merami?" "Yes she leads worship at this church". Or you would hear, " Meramita? O si la que canta?" I wasn't known for my Bible knowledge or my Bible Study classes. I was known for singing and leading worship on Sundays. So it was so hard for me to accept that I couldn't sing. Even much more when I was asked why I was not singing or leading worship during my recovery season.

It may have been a hard time I faced, but It was necessary. I had to face it to grow in my faith and my relationship with God. It tested my faith and my trust in God. I now no longer stress about who I am. I believe who God says I am. I have also learned to accept my sound, my voice. I remind myself of what God has done for me and did for me during that time. I don't need or have ever wanted the fame and spotlight to serve Him. For me it's about the souls that come to encounter His presence and be transformed and forever changed. I am His vessel and it is all for His glory! It's all for the audience of 1. He is the one who has given me the gift, has anointed me and has chosen me for this!. God gets all the honor and glory!

CHAPTER 10
Wonderfully Complex

"Thank you for making me so wonderfully complex"
Psalm 139:14 NLT

Growing up my mom would always tell me "Tu no eres cualquier persona. Eres única". Which translates to "You are not just anyone, you're unique." Me? Unique? Yes! My mom always made sure I knew I was not like everyone else. She saw something in me, something special. When I wanted to follow the crowd, she would repeat it, you're not like everyone else. You're different. I didn't like to hear it, but she's right. I'm not like everyone else. There has always been something in me, about me that makes me unique. I have been the one kept and sheltered more than my siblings. My siblings think I'm the spoiled one. I beg to differ. That title or I should say that role belonged to my oldest brother. I may or may not have shared the role, but we both have been the ones who my parents worried about most. I'm the youngest of my siblings.

I'll never forget one night, I was in my early twenties and I asked my mom why am I different? I was having a hard time understanding why? She responded, "You feel and see things differently. You go through so much because you are strong and pure to face it." She's right. I do feel things differently. I do care about my family and my close friends. It takes a lot for me to let a friendship go. I will give you so many chances to see if you come around but if I see that you won't, I will let you go and move on. Note to keep in mind: Not everyone you meet or encounter will stay with you in your journey.

I may be a friendly person and a loyal friend to those close to me, but I have felt alone. This being "unique" can come with feeling lonely. Feeling like you don't belong because you're different, you're not like everyone else, can be and feel like you're in competition with those who are in the same ministry as you. I know it was something I had to face and deal with and I have learned to accept it. I am still, yes, still learning to embrace my uniqueness. It's a daily struggle to not be so concerned with what others think about me or how they see me. I struggle with being accepted. I struggle with dialing down or hiding my uniqueness from others because I've been told I can be a lot to handle or too needy.

Even at one point, with my siblings, it was a lonely journey for me. I get it. They have kids and families to look after. I'm the least of their worries. But it hurts to think that you're the sibling who is not where everyone else is in their journey. You're not at their level. You're stuck and you feel like you will never get out of the pit.

I didn't always want to have kids. I felt it wasn't for me. I still want to get married. For a long time I felt like kids weren't in my future. Eventually, things changed for me. I realized that changed when my twin sister had her first child. I was so happy on that day, that my love for children and a desire to get married and have my own increased in me.

My twin sister has 3 precious children who I love with my whole heart and would do anything for them. It is different when your "womb-mate" has children of their own. My two older brothers have kids as well, but it's a different kind of special bond with my twin sisters' kids.

I don't know exactly when I will get married or have kids, but I have hope. Some days are harder than others to have hope and faith that it will happen. There have been some rough nights with tears on my pillow as I cry myself to sleep. Sometimes I don't want to wake up in the morning because I want to wallow in my self pity. When you hear it all the time, "hang in there, wait a little longer, it will happen. Don't lose faith!" It's hard not to lose hope.

All in all, I am happy for what my friends and family have accomplished in their personal lives. I got to see my older brothers and twin sister get married and have their own children. I am an auntie of 11 and a great auntie of 1. I'm the cool single auntie.

I am really happy I got to see and be alongside Christine, when she married her Prince Charming and with being one of her bridesmaids. I was asked recently while talking with Marysa that if I was married and had kids and lived the life I have always wanted, would I still want something else? or would I be okay with life and live it to the fullest? A part of me wanted to say I'll be okay with life and a part of me wanted to say, I want more! Is it wrong that I want more in life?

There is a sense of regret in my journey. I regret allowing fear and lies I believed about myself stop me from accomplishing simple goals. For stopping me from taking risks in making decisions in life that could have changed my life and or ministry. I've sheltered myself because of fear and disbelief in my own ability to succeed. I believed the lie of I'm not worth anything and I will always be alone.No longer is that the case. I stand in the truth of God's word for me.

In this season of my life. I am learning to continue to trust in God's perfect timing. He is never late or early, He's always on time. I'm in no rush for marriage. I want to value my time and the people in my life. I'm at the point in my life where I understand that not everyone in your life is meant to stay a lifetime, some are with you for a part of your journey and it's okay to let them go.

This book is an amazing accomplishment. There were days and nights where I wanted to delete it all. I cried so much writing my story. This truly has been a cathartic process and experience. When I wanted to give up and quit writing, I kept reminding myself that this will not be unfinished. This book will be written and published in due time. I didn't want to start this and not finish like most things in my life.

Trying to date someone in your late 30s is not easy. I am traumatized. I am also very oblivious to the dating scene. I don't know how to have a conversation with a guy unless I feel comfortable doing so. I have been told that I can be stand-offish and sometimes too upfront but it is only because I don't know what I am doing or what to say.

I was a lot younger when I had my first boyfriend. My very first serious relationship was when I was 17 years old. It was my junior year in high school and let's face it, I wanted a boyfriend because it was a popular thing. I had crushes on some of my guy friends that they didn't know about. My childhood crush was in a serious relationship and I missed the train on that one.

One Friday night after our youth service I met, for privacy reasons, we will name him, J.D. He was good friends with a mutual friend. He was tall and somewhat lean with slick straight blonde-brown hair. He was a preacher, he was in charge of his HS Bible club. He was a senior in high school, drove a truck, family oriented, loved Jesus with all his heart and soul. I was not even close to where he was spiritually but we both had a relationship with Jesus. He was more "Spiritual" than I was. He was so spiritual that for our first month anniversary, we went to a prayer service. I didn't want to go. I wanted to go see a movie, a rom com, or a candlelit dinner or walking around town holding hands. I didn't want to go to a prayer service. My relationship with J.D. went by fast. By our 4th month of dating, we took pictures. Yep we took those couple pictures, the ones you normally take when you're gonna get engaged. We matched our outfits light blue and black. I wore a light blue sweater with black slacks and my hair down curled with light makeup and a soft color pink lipstick. He wore a light blue sweater and some black dockers with his hair combed back. We gave those pictures to our friends and family. When we broke up, I threw the photos away along with the CD he recorded love songs for me. Years later, I was visiting a friend at her workplace and saw that one of her coworkers, (our former youth pastor), had the exact same picture of J.D. and I. I was so surprised he kept it all those years.

When J.D. and I dated, we spent the "major couple holidays" together. Thanksgiving, Christmas, New Years, Valentine's Day, we spent it together by going to each other's house with our families. On one of the holidays, Christmas, we went to the movies with his sister and brother-in-law. I don't remember which movie we saw. I kept looking at him during the movie, and wasn't paying too much attention to it. My eyes were on my love. I tried to hug him and hold his hands and play with his hair and he wouldn't let me. He would tell me it's not right we are in a public place and people can see us. My response, it's dark and everyone is watching the movie. J.D. wasn't too affectionate in public. He liked to cuddle and hug me but not in public. He wouldn't even hold my hand. He did all that when we were alone like in the car or on the couch but would stop if someone would see us. We never kissed. We would hug and hold hands. I would lay on his chest on the couch but we never kissed. His response to that was always that he was shy and he didn't want to make out unless it was something serious and we would spend our lives together in the future. What?? That kind of rejection messed me up and made me feel like I was not worth loving. It made me feel like he didn't find me beautiful or I was not good enough for him.

During our relationship we broke up a few times. The first time was when he was asked about us and he told the person who asked us that he didn't want to be in a relationship with me. When I asked him about it, he denied it. I was so hurt I didn't want to hear him tell me why he said what he did. In fact, till this day I don't know why. What's worse about that break up is that it was Valentine's Day. We got back together again a year after that break up. He was getting ready to go on a mission trip to Nicaragua. We would still talk on the phone here and there. He told me that he still wanted to make it work between us and see where it would lead. We came to the conclusion of staying together while he was still away on his trip.

While I was in the MC Program, I received a call from J.D. on my birthday. I was so excited to hear from him. My love called me on my special day. I was so happy! However, our conversation was not a pleasant one. Once again I was heartbroken. He told me the long distance wasn't working out for him and he found someone while he was on his trip and he is falling for her and doesn't know how he feels about me and he still cares about me but needs time to think about what he wants. I tried so hard to not let that ruin my birthday but I cried after we hung up. That night, my roommate planned a small birthday party with the MC friends and staff at a Mexican restaurant. I may have been surrounded by people but I felt so alone. I didn't have my family or my close friends there for my 19th birthday, and my heart was in pieces again. I appreciated the gesture from my roommate, but all I really wanted was to be surrounded by my family and loved ones. Like when we were younger and although my dad's job was demanding as a fireman, he would take all of us to a day at the lake in Del Rio, Texas. If we were not with my dad, my sister and I were with my mom helping at the church we grew up in while living in Texas.

J.D. is part of the reason I have trust issues with men. My final break up with J.D. was during the time I worked at a call center. He had visited the church I went to on a Sunday and he was waiting for me at the exit door after the service. We talked for a bit after church and he told me he wanted to have lunch with me. I told him I'll call him. I did call the next day but not for "our lunch date" but because I was left stranded at work and needed a ride to the apartment complex I lived at the time. I needed a big favor and he came to help me. He picked me up in his blue pickup truck. He leaned over and unlocked the door to my side and I got in. I gave him a hug and told him thank you. We drove to Arden Fair Mall in Sacramento, CA. We had lunch at Panda Express. I don't remember what he ordered or what I ordered. The memory is a bit vague. After we ate, he took me home. I invited him into the apartment and we were alone. As he was sitting on the couch, I wanted to make out with him but something held me back. I fought the urge of just making out with him like we see in the movies and having sex with him. If I had given into having sex with him, my "good girl" image would have been destroyed. I am so glad that Nothing happened between us.

J.D. got up, grabbed his jacket and I opened the front door to the apartment and he walked out. At that moment, I thought I would never see him again and that I missed my chance at love and possibly marriage. Well, it was probably a few years later that I saw him again. This time our encounter was so different. I was invited to go to a

Sunday church service with one of my friends who later became a roommate. She was attending her uncle's church . We arrived at the church and we sat in the middle of the front section. I was enjoying the service during worship, when it was time for the offering to be picked up, the Pastor asked one of the deacons to come to the front to pray for the offering and who was the deacon, it was him. J.D. His reaction to me being there was one of shock and confusion and he turned red and nervous. I waved at him from my seat. He prayed for the offering and went to his seat and sat down. The pastor then tells the congregation to get out of our seats and say hi to one another in the church. J.D. avoided saying hi to me. He went to the other side of the church to greet the members sitting on the side where he was. I turned around and greeted the woman who was sitting in back of me. The woman was J.D.'s wife. He had gotten married. A punch to my gut! He was married, and he looked happily married! I don't know if he is still married. He went back to where we both were, his wife and I and he casually introduced me to her. I told him, we just met, I told her who I was. I told her I was his ex-girlfriend. He looked so stunned that I would tell her that. He was not too happy about it.

After church, he asked me what I was doing there and that it was so uncomfortable for me to be there. I told him I was just as uncomfortable as he was and surprised to see him there with his wife. He was my first boyfriend. I cared about him and loved him but I was not in love with him. Maybe I was? It was more of the idea of having a boyfriend that I loved.

It took a very long time, years for me to try another relationship. My last relationship was recent. January 2020. It lasted almost 3 months. I really thought this was it for me. This relationship was not what I had hoped for. I met Sebastian (whose name has been changed to protect privacy) on a Christian website called United Young. I usually don't like to meet men on those sites, but I decided to give it a try. On December 24th of 2019 I was going to cancel my subscription when I saw a message from Sebastian with his phone number on it. I wrote down his phone number on an index card. I responded to his message and gave him my phone number that day. We texted daily for a couple of weeks. Then we talked on the phone and he said he wanted to see where the relationship would lead. I agreed. I enjoyed our texting and then getting to hear his voice and talking to him on the phone for the first time after a couple of weeks of texting back and forth, it seemed way too fast than what I'd expected. His voice was sweet and a bit raspy. One day, I went outside to the back part of the house where my window was. He called me on his lunch break and I was so nervous and shaky, I froze. My knees locked as I stood outside my window and as I tried to walk into the yard, with my red pantuflas (slippers) he said, "I'm here for something real, I will never hurt you or break your heart. You can trust me." I believed him. When he said that, I stood there stunned because he said what I wanted to hear. I, too, didn't want to play games or hurt him. I wanted to be in this relationship and see the possibility of something that would last for a long time. Longer than the almost 3 months it lasted. I hung up the phone with him and smiled thinking this can be a potential relationship.

The couple of months of getting to know him was where I got to know about his job and his family. He lived with his mom and younger half brother. He is the man of the house. Sebastian takes care of the house and his mother and brother who is Autistic. He has a sibling in Nicaragua. Sebastian doesn't speak or have a great relationship with his father. That's what I found out because he told me. I noticed one time while on the phone, he would not treat his brother in a caring way. He was very impatient with him and I didn't like that too much. When I called him out on it, he told me to let him handle his brother and not worry because his brother needs to learn how to show respect. I didn't like the tone he used. I ignored it and kept getting to know him. The more I would get to know him and talk on the phone with him, the more warning signs would show up that I did not want to see. He was impatient, rude, his mom handled his expenses, he had no respect for his leadership at church. He did not want to attend a Pentecostal Christian church.

When I told him I was writing a book, he would make it about him and would make me feel like I was competing with him. He would get upset when I could not talk to him. He lived in Georgia, I lived in California. The long distance was a bit of a struggle but I did the best I could to talk to him and when I couldn't he made me feel guilty for not being available to speak to him. He would tell me that I didn't care about him and he is a needy person and needs attention or he gets mad. Yep so true. I was not used to the clingy side of him. At times I felt like I was the **man** in the relationship. I was starting to no longer be interested in him. He became too possessive. He would not like that I had friends and I would hang out with them or talk to them on the phone. He wanted to be #1 in my life and I couldn't give that place to him. He even told me one time, "When we get married, you're gonna only have friends that I approve of" and would laugh after saying that. I didn't find that funny. That scared me. The thought of me not being able to talk to my friends from California scared me. I got so scared that I did a background check on him.

There are still a lot of things that I didn't agree with that he would say or do, but for the sake of privacy and me blocking it out, it is not worth mentioning. Our break up was so overwhelming and exhausting. Sebastian not only showed me his possessive side but his angry side. He would yell on the phone and would make me feel bad for not giving him the attention he wanted. I got emotionally drained that I could no longer be in that relationship. I asked him for a breather and some space. I didn't tell him for how long, in my mind it would be at least a month. I needed to reevaluate my life and my feelings about him. Is this what I want? Do I want to be trapped in a relationship with someone who gets easily hurt and cannot handle when I speak up for myself? I want a partner with purpose. Sad to say, I was not seeing that in Sebastian. I couldn't handle it anymore. He made it worse with his attitude and how he acted when I asked him for space. When we broke up for good, he took me off his social media. He didn't call me after that last conversation coming back from our space period. No explanation. No text, he definitely ended our relationship millennial style. I even tried to call him but no answer. I texted him and got no response. It was over! I was hurt but also relieved, at one point, he and I had talked about marriage, we talked about kids. We were going to meet in person in July of 2020. We broke up in April of 2020.

Before we had our first fight, he told me he had a ring picked out and he would ask for my hand in marriage when he would come and meet me in person. I now know that I would have not accepted the proposal. This break up made me realize what I really want and need. I want a person who can be an encouragement to my purpose. A purpose partner. One who I can grow with and learn from. One that has a purpose of their own and is willing to walk alongside me with mine and I with his. I don't want someone I would have to walk on eggshells to protect his feelings or my feelings. I want someone who can tell me the truth where neither of us feel offended but feel pushed to do better to be better. I want someone who loves God before they can love me.

I wonder if that person is out there? One day I will find out who he is. I want that, and I believe I can and will have that. I need to continue to work on myself and heal from hurts and things in my life that have stopped me on my journey. There are still things in my life that are unfinished, which over the years, I felt like a failure, incapable, inadequate because I have still yet to accomplish a few goals. One major goal and you may think it's the simplest thing, I don't have my driver's license. I can drive a car, but I have been afraid to take the driving test and fail because I have failed it numerous times. However, it is something I am currently working on. This time, I have the drive to get this accomplished. I know I will accomplish what is unfinished! I have learned (still learning) to accept and embrace where I am now and the journey I have traveled in life. This book itself has been a journey. An accomplishment that I honestly didn't think I would finish.

I don't know what God has for me in the future, but I believe that it will be beyond what I have dreamt and even expected. Maybe your story is not similar to mine or maybe it is. We all have our own story, our own journey. Our story, our journey matters. God will use it for His purpose, His glory. We don't have to have it all together. He will make something beautiful out of ashes, out of our mistakes, our failures, our shortcomings He takes all that and creates beautiful things. We are those beautiful things!

I share my journey, my memoir to remind you it's okay to not always have it figured out. It's okay to not be where everyone else is. That's what makes us unique is our different stories, and journeys. I can smile and be grateful for my life and what I have learned through the many blessings and experiences I have lived through this far. Who am I?? I am a woman with a story of finding herself in her life journey. Finding her identity. I know who I am. I am one who has been broken and left out, abandoned and rejected, however that doesn't determine who I am. I have learned to trust God and forgive not just myself but those who have tried to break me time and time again. My identity is only in God. I no longer question why I am who I am. I have gained confidence in Him and when I feel like I have no purpose, like I don't belong, like I'm not loved, I remember my journey. I remember how far I have come and I'm still here!

I am a woman who is misunderstood, affectionate, remarkable, trustworthy, honorable, and a bit assured of herself (still working on that). That's who I am. I am the friend you can call in the middle of the night and will be there for you. I love with all my heart. I give generously. I speak the truth and listen carefully. I don't judge you if you make mistakes but I help you heal and restore. If you do me wrong, I won't hold it against you. I will just keep my distance. I will still say hi when I see you, just know that it won't be the same kind of trust as before. My family is so dear to my heart. I love my Texas family as well as my California family. They will always be my foundation, my roots. I am a proud Tex-Mexican woman from a small town, Eagle Pass. My childhood memories are there along with some memories here in California. I grew up here in California, and I'm still here in the city where I grew up.

I am looking forward to what's next. I don't know what God still has for me. I don't know if soon I'll meet the man of God I've prayed for. Will I still be living in California or will I move to another state or go back to Texas? All I know is that it is going to be a beautiful mess! No life or story is perfect. Each and every day we are being formed by the potter's hands. We may not know what He is making and the process may not be comfortable and the stretching hurts but the Potter knows what a masterpiece we will have after we are placed in the fires of life.

Who am I? I am Merami, one who is wonderfully complex.

Thank You!

First and foremost, God, *thank you for your love, peace and grace. I remember having the dream you gave me to write this book and I asked you for courage and strength and peace. This book would have not been possible without the leading and guidance of your Holy Spirit to share my story on this platform. It is Yours! Use this for Your glory. Amen.*

Mom & Dad- For your love and support and for raising me in the truth of God's Word and showing me to serve Jesus with all my heart.

My two older brothers and twin sister

Jesse- You loved me in a special way that left an imprint in my heart. You supported me in the best way a big brother could . I love you and miss you every day! I know you're proud of me and watching me from heaven grow and succeed.

Carlos- Chacho! Thank you for loving me and supporting me in everything I do. You always make sure your little sis is okay and is there to help in any way possible. OMG! Your little sister wrote a book!

Mary- My first bestie. My womb mate. My twin sister, God knew I needed you to walk through life hand-in-hand. You are a rock, a strength in my life. The lessons I've learned from you are endless, always showing me something new and inspiring me to be strong and resilient like you! Thank you for your support, love and friendship. I am so blessed to be your little sister. Love you so much!

Nieces and Nephews- Mis Amores, you light up my world and bring happiness to my heart. Tia Shorty loves you and will always be here for you.

Familia en Texas y Wisconsin- Los quiero muchísimo con todo mi corazón. Gracias por su apoyo siempre y por creer en este sueño ser se una realidad.

California Family- *Thank you for the good times and memories shared. I will cherish them forever.*

Christine Correa Butler- *This book would have not been possible if it wasn't for your support. Thank you for creating my aesthetic writing nook where I was inspired to write my story comfortably. Forever grateful for your support.*

Damaris Serrato- *My friend, your words of encouragement through some hard times during my writing process are forever appreciated. Thank you for pushing me to have hard conversations to heal and be restored in the midst of them. Thank you for keeping me accountable when I did not want to be in ministry. Thank you for reminding me to never let anything or anyone stop me from walking in the calling God has given me and to never neglect my gift. Love you.*

Marysa Garcia- *My Reeses! Thank you for helping me through my journey. Your input on this book really helped me dig deep in myself and be vulnerable to share my story. You're an amazing friend who has been there since our teenage years, adulthood and during the time when I began to write this book. I appreciate you so much for being there to discuss my heart on the book and what I wanted to say. Thank you a million. Love you.*

Paola Johnson- *Our conversations about life and Jesus are my favorite things about our friendship, sisterhood. Many conversations with you have left me inspired and challenged to love like Jesus. Thank you for praying with me and for me as I wrote my story. Thank you for believing in me and reminding me that I am a writer, a story teller. Te quiero my friend, mi hermana.*

Johna Hill- *(from Jae Consulting Inc). My friend, my sister, my editor. Truly a Godsend. This story could have not been told, expressed in my voice without your help through prayer, editing sessions, and guidance from the Holy Spirit. Thank you for believing in me and my story to be shared with you and el mundo entero. OMG!! I am a writer! Thank you for helping me with the publishing process! You're the best!! Love you sister.*

Lissette Rodriguez- *Thank you for loving me like one of your own and for welcoming me into your family. The Correas will always be so dear to my heart. Thank you for making sure I was ok even when you moved from NorCal. Your words of love and wisdom you shared with me will forever be imprinted in my heart. I learned so much from you the time I worked at the NPLAD offices. You taught me to do the best at everything that I do, and to never give up trying to achieve my goals in life. This Tex-Mex girl loves you so much.*

Pastors Chito & Norma Rosado- *It's an honor and blessing to call you friends and be under your leadership. Thank you for your constant prayers and encouragement throughout this project and many years of my journey. Grateful for your lives and your leadership at The Father's House Elk Grove. Thank you! Love you both.*

Pastors Ben & Lyndsey Guerrero.- *It is an honor to serve under your leadership on the Worship Team at The Father's House Elk Grove. So blessed to call you friends. Your heart for Jesus and love for others is beautifully infectious along with your welcoming spirit and encouragement makes it so easy to feel like you're not just a part of a team, but a family. Also, Noble Coffee is amazing! You have me as a friend and customer for life. Love you.*

Chris Serra- *Bro!! Thank you for making the cover of this book and for being a part of the journey. You brought the vision to life and I am so grateful for your work and dedication to this. Thank you!*

Ariel Espinoza- God knew what He was doing when he placed you in my life. Grateful for your friendship. You helped me reach a goal I thought was impossible to reach. You never left my side or let me give up even when I wanted to. I'm so blessed to have you in my life. I love our Jesus and life talks, our hangouts and always so much fun leading with you at The Father's House Elk Grove. Love you friend! "We're Stronger Together!" Siempre!

Mayra Rodriguez- Mi Carnalita novelera. Thank you for being one of the first ones to read the first manuscript before it was edited. Your love and support is forever cherished. Thank you for being an amazing friend. Te quiero mi Carnalita.

Theresa Legaspi- Amiga! Thank you for your loving support and for the good talks at our Women's group and encouragement to write and share my story. My E.P sister te quiero mucho.

Crystal Cantu.- Girl we go back from our youth days at ECC to now serving together at The Father's House Elk Grove. Thank you so much for being an incredible friend who has shown me to have someone's back and be there through thick and thin as well as to serve with a cheerful heart. So thankful for our reconnection in the season I wrote this book. You, my friend, are amazing.

Edith & Jonathan Wax.- Thank you for encouraging me and asking me about how this journey was going. Thank you for our talks about life and growing in Jesus, I appreciate you and I am blessed to call you friends.

Sara Valdez.- You pushed me and believed in me when I needed to reach a goal in my life. Thank you for your encouragement and for not giving up on me when I wanted to give up on that goal. We all need a little push from Sara in our lives! Love you my friend.

Victoria Quiñones- *Thank you for being a wonderful friend. Thank you for your wisdom and encouraging support. Thank you for believing in me and the gifts inside me to be who I am today. Love you so much.*

Ana G. Schmitt- *Thank you for always checking in to see how I am truly doing and offering to help me be more organized and keep momentum in my life. So blessed by your friendship. I am so grateful that we have been reunited and are now serving at The Father's House Elk Grove. Love you my friend.*

Gabriela Cisneros- *Gaby! Wow, we have known each other for a long time. You are family! Love you like a sister. Thank you for being a good friend. Thank you for the hangouts and talks throughout the years. I love you my friend. Thank you for being a part of this project with the decorations for the book release party.*

My CRC Choir Buddies: *Vanessa & Sam, thank you for being great friends all these years and for your insight on life and relationships. Love our dinner dates and fun conversations and spilling the tea about our favorite celebrities and our top 5 favorite male actors, I appreciate you both for being there through hard times and good times*

Pamela Praniuk Romero- *I remember my first vocal lesson with you, I left that lesson wanting to learn more and grow more. Years later, still taking lessons with you and I keep learning and growing. You are not just my vocal coach, you are a dear friend. I appreciate your words of love and encouragement to keep up with my vocal care and exercise daily. You believed in my gift since my first lesson with you and for that I am forever grateful. Thank you for pushing me beyond my abilities to grow in my craft, my gift. Love you my friend.*

Diana Garcia-Johnson- *Amiga, thank you for being one of the first ones to hear the beginning pages of my writing. Thank you for your encouraging words and for showing me it is okay to serve Jesus even in our mess. I appreciate our coffee and dinner dates of sharing struggles, and victories and us dancing in your car to classic R&B music. "We, both Hood and Holy". Love you Amiga.*

Naty Medina- *Thank you for believing in me. Thank you for giving me input on the first couple of chapters and challenging me to tell my story authentically. Thank you, for our talks, your encouragement. Love you my friend.*

Linda Medina- *My first friend when I first arrived at ECC in Sacramento. Your friendship is a blessing and encouragement to never give up but move forward as we trust in Jesus to get us to the other side. I love you my friend, my sister.*

Jessica Delgado- *Prima! Thank you for being a part of this journey and project. Thank you for taking my pictures and for capturing my story beautifully. Love you!*

Momma Rosado- *Muchas gracias por sus oraciones y apoyo en este proyecto. Gracias por amarme como una hija. La quiero mucho.*

Brandee Winter- *Thank you for being a part of my journey and for being a friend I can count on for support in sharing my story.*

Rachel Malott- *My MC Roomie! If it wasn't for you literally throwing the bible at me, I would not be where I am today. So blessed to call you friend and sister in Christ. I thank God for your friendship. Our conversations and connection always leave me encouraged and strengthened.*

Bianca Juarez- *Friend! Thanks for believing in me to finish my first chapter of this book. Your ministry is a blessing to my life. Aye! Twin power!*

Trinity Anderson- *Amiga! Thank you for sharing your experiences and wisdom with me about being a worship leader as well. Your amistad and sisterhood is a blessing, a gift in my life. Thank you for always encouraging all of us to stay the course. God is building faith again! He is Moving! Love you mi Amiga, mi hermana.*

Yvonne Muñoz- *Amiga! So blessed by your friendship. Thank you for your words of life, and for your prayers. Love you un monton!*

Belen Godina- *Amiga! Aprecio mucho nuestra amistad. Gracias por las pláticas mientras me arreglabas mi cabello y por las convivencias con café y rica comida . Gracias por tu confianza y apoyo te quiero mucho amiga.*

Cristine Cantu- *Thank you for being a sister and friend. It is always fun being on stage with you on Sundays at TFH Elk Grove. Your strength and tenacity to do and be better is so inspiring. Keep serving and working for the Kingdom. Love you sis.*

To my TFH Elk Grove Sisters from Women's Group- *Thank you for sharing your heart and wisdom with me. Thank you for praying with me on this project.*

I am blessed to know and do life with each and every one of you.

MEET THE AUTHOR

Merami, born in Eagle Pass Texas, and grew up in Sacramento, California. She attended Centro Cristiano Ebenezer, now known as The Avenue Church Sacramento, where at the age of 19, she first experienced the call of God in her life to lead others into the presence of God. She then felt led to attend a Discipleship Program for 2 years in Northern Washington where she studied and received her certificate of completion of 1 year through Global University.

During her time in the Discipleship Program, she was given the opportunity to lead worship at outreaches and churches in the 4 corners of the state of Washington. When she returned to Northern California, she led Worship at services and conferences and was also a part of a traveling Worship team for a period of 2 years, Double Portion, while serving at Cantico Nuevo, now known as New Season Español in Elk Grove, CA.

Merami is currently pursuing a degree in Ministerial Studies at Epic Bible Institute. She is now a part of The Dream Team of a newly launched church plant; The Father's House Elk Grove. A church led by close pastoral friends in the city of Elk Grove, where she also serves on the Worship Team.

Contact info:
Instagram: @Truly.merami
Email: Truly.merami@gmail.com

TESTIMONIALS

"Who am I" is a must read and easy page turner. It is an introspective look of one writer's life who shares candid experiences of what it is like to be a Worship Leader on and off the stage. The ups and the downs of finding one's spiritual self in a world full of noise. This is not only the
story of Merami but it is the story of so many of us as believers as we have fought to navigate through this world while upholding our beliefs and values. It is the story of using our God given platform(s) for His Glory!
Johna R. Hill

Who Am I really reaches your heart and reminds you that you are not alone. It's not just relatable to worship leaders or people in ministry but anyone can relate to it on a human level and spiritual level. This memoir is a beautiful story of life and all the highs and lows that come with it, along with the importance of keeping God at the center of it all. It's a reminder to never lose hope or faith in God even in your darkest moments. It also depicts how normal and human it is to have fears, and self-doubt, and to question your purpose or calling, or self-worth and to even question God sometimes. It's a great example of how much we need God and family and good friends to help us overcome hardships and losses throughout life. Struggling with identity and discovering who you are is a heavy process that is showcased so well in this memoir. I really loved the honesty and vulnerability which showed so much strength. Most importantly this story will inspire others to not give up, to keep fighting through pain and struggles, to hold onto hope and onto God and who He made us to be, and to always remember we are not alone. Thank you for reminding me I am not alone.

Mayra Rodriguez

So proud of Merami for stepping out to document her journey this way! Pleasantly surprised that I personally relate to so much of her story in detail of growing up with this calling as well as knowing that I'm not alone in bearing the tough seasons that led to the resilience I walk in today. God is desiring a remnant of strong Worship Leaders who understand the weight of the assignment and the value of bringing our whole selves to the table for His will and His glory. Praying that this book blesses and inspires each reader to stay the course and see it through with an ever present YES on their heart.

Trinity Anderson, Worship Leader, Redemption Church San Jose CA.

"Merami lives a life of worship on and off the stage and with decades of experience under her belt, she knows what it means to sing a new song to the Lord in every season. I pray that this book blesses you as much as it blessed me!"

Lyndsey Guerrero, Worship Pastor, The Father's House Elk Grove

CONGRATULATIONS Merami!! I really enjoyed this book! I laughed, I was briefly sad and shocked all at the same time. I thought this book was encouraging regardless of what level we are in our spiritual walk. Your perseverance through life difficulties and challenges is both inspiring and an example of how we can do and get through anything with King Jesus.

The book is easy to understand. It incorporates personal examples, scriptures, and a testimony of grace, and mercy Jesus died to give us. I recommend this book for anyone who needs healing from brokenness and inspiration regardless of what stage you are in your spiritual journey.

You overcame so many trials and setbacks and never turned away from God. I am grateful for having you as my lifelong friend and I'm looking forward to you signing my book!

Crystal Cantu

Who Am I? Is a story of someone that had every reason to give up and walk away from all that God had in store for her, but she chose to follow Him anyway. I am so glad Merami didn't give up. I have known Merami for many years and I can say this, that she is the real deal. God uses her in such a powerful way. If you are looking to be inspired and encouraged, this book is for you. May this book remind you that God never makes mistakes.

Chito Rosado, Lead Pastor of The Father's House Elk Grove